First C
(A Commander Steadfast Thriller)

Richard Freeman

Table of Contents

All the men on the ships in this story are fictitious, as are the convoy and escort ships. Almost every incident is, though, based on a true event in one of the thousands of convoys during the Second World War.

Chapter 1 - The New Captain

Chief Petty Officer Reg Phillips, his cap pushed back at a jaunty angle, sat foursquare on an upturned crate on the deck of HMS *Defiant*. Through the clouds of white smoke emerging from his filthy looking pipe he eyed the lanky young redhead who was nonchalantly walking up the gangway. The newcomer had the air of a man who was already at home on the ship. This will be the new Sparks, Phillips said to himself.

George Barton flung down his brand new kit bag onto the deck and, without a hint of deference, nodded a half-greeting to Phillips.

'You're to take over from Ted?' Phillips asked.

'That's right.'

'Good luck to you then. He never had any.'

'Why?'

'Never you mind. We've worse things to worry about.'

'Worse?'

'It's the captain's first ship.'

'So what?'

'Where've you been? Don't you know it's bad luck to be on a captain's first ship?'

'I don't believe in that sort of stuff.'

'Just wait and see. You new to destroyers?'

'New to ships, actually.'

'Well, welcome aboard the roughest posting in the Navy. We get all the dirty jobs: shadowing Jerry, chasing off E-boats, hunting down subs. And if they can't think of any other way to send us to the bottom, there's always minelaying. Then there's fog and mines even when Jerry's not about.'

'And this trip?'

'Coal-scuttle brigade, or coastal convoy to you. Offers every 'azard you can wish for: mines, torpedoes, Stukas, rocks and shoals.'

'He's right,' came a voice from behind Barton. 'Joe Callaghan, Gunner's Mate. I've been on the Artic run, the Atlantic run and the

Gibraltar run to Alex. Sunk three times. But guess which is the worst berth I've ever had.'

Barton looked quizzical.

'This one – the bloody East Coast convoys. A total, hellish, living nightmare.'

Barton, young, naïve, and excited at the prospect of going to sea, would have liked to hear more, but Phillips interrupted the discussion with a curt, 'You'd better look sharp. The new captain will be here soon.'

Callaghan nodded a silent 'follow me' and took Barton below, leaving Phillips sucking on his grimy pipe. Thickset and only five feet eight inches tall, Phillips was a solid looking man. His profuse and rather ragged black beard and his full head of matching hair gave the impression of someone not to be argued with. He was a Navy man to his roots, having enlisted before the Great War when the Service was the nation's pride. In June 1911 he had stood to attention on the deck of *Dreadnought* as she sailed past the *Royal Yacht* at the Coronation Fleet Review, where he had saluted King George V and Churchill, who was then First Lord of the Admiralty. Five years later, in May 1916, still on *Dreadnought*, he took part in the Battle of Jutland. He claimed to have seen *Invincible* sink, but many treated that as a legitimate embellishment of an old sailor's memories.

Thirty years in the Navy! No man could have been prouder of the Senior Service, nor more committed to making his own ship worthy of the Navy's great traditions. A Chief Petty Officer of five years' standing, Phillips was a man set in his ways. Or rather, the Navy's ways. The ship and the men were everything to him. Woe betide the man in his cups on shore who dared to say a word against her. Phillips would defend *Defiant* to the last.

He had seen them all: the slackers, the know-alls, the men over-eager for promotion before their time, and the plain insubordinate. But he only warmed to men like himself: down-to-earth, loyal and steady. No fuss, no show. Just keep the ship running and keep your head down, he would tell the new recruits. If they did, Phillips would always be there to support and defend them. The rest could look after themselves. As to Barton, he wasn't too sure about him – rather too much on the cocky side, he thought.

Phillips soon forgot about Barton and turned his thoughts to the change of captain. Smith, or Old Smithy as he was affectionately known, had been taken off with appendicitis when *Defiant* had returned from her last convoy two days ago. Now *there* was a captain to Phillips's liking; easy-going, he left Phillips to sort the men out his own way. The thing about Smithy was that he had no ambition: he had come out of retirement for the war and couldn't wait to get back to his small-holding in the Cotswolds. He'd rather talk about his cows and pigs than the war and the Navy. But would the new captain be another Smithy, or one of those difficult types who are all ambition and medal-hunting, he asked himself. That soon upset a ship – and Phillips.

***

An hour later, Phillips was still enjoying his captain-free possession of the ship as he drew on his pipe and sucked in a mouthful of stale air. Lifting one leg over the other, he deftly knocked out the ash with three sharp taps on his boot. As he reached into his pocket for his tobacco pouch, the sound of the grinding gears of an ancient taxi crawling along the congested dockside broke his reverie. Only when the vehicle drew up rather sharply at some distance from the ship did Phillips realise what this signified: the new captain.

Lieutenant Commander George Steadfast RNR nearly tore the rear door of the taxi off its hinges as he flung it open and bounded out. He took two steps forward and then stopped and quizzically looked around for his ship. Once he was sure which battle-scarred heap of metal was his, he edged around the large puddles of black oily water and stepped over coils of wire, ripped out cables, mangled metal, and boxes of stores that were littering the dockside. Meanwhile, his taxi driver dumped a mountain of cases and boxes at the foot of the gangway.

Leaving his luggage on the dockside, Steadfast walked slowly towards the ship, not with the ambling walk of a casual onlooker, but with the slow, deliberate walk of an inspectorial mind. Before boarding, he paused at the foot of the gangway to admire his new command. She had clearly seen the wars. In places, rust burst through her peeling paint; in others patched up steelwork gleamed with new camouflage. But she was a beauty: small, yes, but streamlined and sleek. Already he could feel her racing through the pounding waves, spray tumbling over her foredeck, the white foamy sea streaming behind. At last he was to command on the bridge. No longer would he be held back by timid commanders or lambasted by fault-finding captains. His pulse quickened at the thought of the throbbing engines, the thundering guns, and the acrid smell of cordite.

Steadfast was short – about the only quality that he shared with his Chief Petty Officer. He had a powerful, square face with a wry snarling curl to his lips. He walked with his head tipped back that bit farther than was customary and eyed all those he met with a quizzical, disdainful air. His short, dark hair and clean shaven chin gave him a businesslike appearance. His haughty voice matched his demeanour, especially when he barked out orders in a crisp 'do it now' manner. Many who met Steadfast saw in him a fearful mixture of the supercilious 'Jacky' Fisher and the arrogant David Beatty. He would not have demurred from either characterisation.

Steadfast had joined the Navy after the First World War and worked his way up to lieutenant, but the endless cut-backs following the Washington Naval Treaty of 1922 had left few chances for commands. In 1933 he left the Navy and started his own art gallery in Bond Street. It did well and by the time war broke out it had a reliable reputation for sea and naval pictures. His passion for artwork was equalled only by his passion for hunting. Whenever possible he would retreat to his tiny cottage in the depths of rural Leicestershire to spend the weekend ripping through the countryside on his hunter, which brought him the same thrill and sense of triumph as did the search for an enemy submarine or the chase of a warship.

But Steadfast had not honed his naval skills to spend this war showing seascapes and battle scenes to people with enough money to keep themselves out of the war. And, in any case, fox hunting was suspended for the duration. All in all, he welcomed the war. For him it offered a chance of fame and glory. He imagined himself conning a zigzagging warship under attack from Stuka dive bombers or patiently following asdic pings as he hunted down U-boats, or even heroically rescuing men from sinking ships. In a few years' time when the war ended – and he hoped that would not be too soon – he saw himself marching down Whitehall in a victory parade with a string of medals on his strutting chest and perhaps dressed in at least a rear admiral's insignia. In short, Steadfast was a man in a hurry, a man on the make.

He had signed-up on the outbreak of war and was quickly appointed lieutenant in the destroyer HMS *Orchard*. It was Narvik in 1940 that taught him what modern war was like. Holed up in that long fiord at the flaming port and under constant air attack, he watched ships such as the H-class destroyer HMS *Hunter* go under. Then there was the agonisingly long retreat home in which the carrier HMS *Glorious* had been sunk. After Narvik he had done a year on HMS *South Riding* as First Lieutenant with the Atlantic convoys. She had gone down one night – torn in two by a single torpedo. Steadfast knew what it was to freeze on a raft in a rough sea, watching the life slip away from your companions, one by agonizing one. He knew what it was to have little hope of seeing the next dawn and the fear that instilled in men. Some survivors, such as Lieutenant Richards and Able Seaman Rigby, had never recovered. They were now broken men, who cowered at the sound of gunfire and woke screaming in the night. Deep down, Steadfast knew that he too carried the mental scars of that ordeal. He still had nightmares when he found himself back on the sinking ship, flames leaping around him, men screaming as the skin was shorn from their bodies, the sea on fire and dead and dying men dotted on the waves. His worst fear was to wake screaming one night in his cot at sea and so reveal his weakness to his men on this new command.

There were more personal reasons for Steadfast's out-and-out determination to deal the enemy as many mortal blows as he could. First there was the murder of his grandmother, at her own breakfast table by the Derfflinger and the Von der Tann when Rear Admiral Franz Hipper had bombarded Scarborough in December 1914. That cowardly act had bitten deep into his soul and drove him forward in moments of weakness. More recently there was the death of his brother at the hands of Korvettenkapitän Johannes Wendorff. It was one of Wendorff's flotilla of E-boats that had sunk the merchant ship on which Raymond had been a naval gunner. Steadfast's greatest ambition was to meet Wendorff and send him and his E-boat to the bottom of the North Sea.

Yes, Steadfast knew about war and he knew its subtle combination of crushing boredom intermingled with terrifying actions. Yet not for one moment did he think of asking for an easier berth. This war was to be the defining moment of his life. It was a test of his manhood – a test he was determined not to fail. So when the order to join *Defiant* came from Vice

Admiral C G Ramsey KCB of the Rosyth Command, he was filled with apprehensive jubilation.

Chapter 2 – Steadfast Takes Command

The *Defiant* was one of the new Hunt class type III escort destroyers. One thousand tons of sleek beauty with a bow that could cut through any sea and a bold bridge abaft her single funnel. Aft she was lean and low. There was not much space to spare on the flats, but that was because she was packed from stem to stern with her fearsome weaponry. She was ready to fend off all comers with her four 4-inch and four 2-pound quick-firing guns and her two recently added Oerlikons on either side of the bridge. She bristled with the latest technology, including radar-controlled direction firing for the guns. Steadfast didn't understand much about all those valves, transformers and tubes, but he knew what they could do. The main armament would be aimed by the amazing box of tricks called the director. All the aimer had to do was to point his telescope at the target for the type 285 radar to pick up the range and direction. Then the magic director sent the details to the guns and they turned to follow the ship's prey.

Coming out of his daydreaming Steadfast sprinted up the gangway. Phillips had just enough time to jump to his feet and salute.

'Welcome aboard, sir!'

'Thank you, er …'

'Philips, sir. I'll have the men put your luggage in your cabin. Number One's in the wardroom. There's tea if you'd like it.'

Philips went below, leaving Steadfast to inspect his ship. As the Chief Petty Officer eased his heavy frame down the ladder, he mused on the arrival of this haughty-looking captain with a bellicose air. He wasn't sure that was what the Navy needed nowadays. Gone were the days when you met the enemy face-to-face and dashed at him with unrestrained bravado. Now death came without warning from an unseen foe. In the depths of the night one unannounced, shattering explosion could send a ship to the bottom in minutes. That required a new type of captain – not fearless, fear was what kept you alert – but strong, resolute and determined on denying the sea to the German menace, without displays of mindless swagger. Would Steadfast know when to attack and when to hold back? The last man got it just right. Smithy never flinched from battle, but nor did he seek out trouble. Now, Phillips feared, the ship was about to be in the hands of a man with no caution at all. 'Just when I've got the ship running like clockwork,' he muttered with all the resignation of an old hand.

As Steadfast turned towards the ladder to go below he noted the furious preparations for sailing. Sides of beef lay on the deck alongside bulging sacks of potatoes, bursting string bags of onions, cabbage and other vegetables. One-hundred-and-seventy men took a lot of feeding. The seamen strained under the weight as they hauled the stores on board and humped them down the ladders to fill every last corner of the ship below.

Other hands worked on the more delicate task of taking on ammunition – the last run had clearly diminished supplies. They handled the bright brass four-inch shells with care, taking them down to the magazines. Those could put up a good fight, Steadfast thought, as he ran his eye over the supplies of armour-piercing shell and shrapnel. Some was set aside for the ready-use lockers on deck.

Now, excited by his new command, Steadfast went aft to watch some depth-charges coming on board. He smiled the smile of a self-satisfied man. This was *his* ship, *his* domain. He turned back towards the ladder and went to meet his officers.

***

'Gin and bitters, please, Steward,' said Captain Steadfast as he entered the wardroom.

'Tell me about the ship, Number One.'

'She's a warhorse, sir,' responded Lieutenant Henry Gardiner RNVR. 'We've only been commissioned for a year. We've done for a Jerry sub and seen off a good many others. Of course, we've had our knocks – been in for dockyard repairs twice, once from shrapnel damage and one collision.'

'So, you're RNVR. What do you do in Civvy Street?'

'Actor, sir. Mostly West End stuff, but there's a bit of touring.'

'Tricky for getting in the water, eh?'

'A bit, but my father-in-law has a small yacht near Harwich. I often get down there on Sundays.'

The condescending look on Steadfast's face was all that Gardiner needed to realise the disdain that Steadfast felt for RNVR officers. But, after over a year of wartime service, he had come to expect this reaction from the career officers.

'And the men?'

'A good lot, sir. They've had a tough time. You know what it's like. You get into dock with plans for a few days off, set foot on dry ground and, hey presto, you're handed orders for the next day. Boiler cleans are our best chance of a bit of leave. But these are all Chatham lads, so leave's not much use when we put in at Rosyth or some other place off the end of the earth. I won't say you need to go easy on the men – that wouldn't be right – but they like to be appreciated. They know they've got a tough job and they like others to acknowledge it. Especially now. We're just back from a bad run. Three colliers lost and some very nasty sights with the deck covered with mangled bodies. It takes it out of the men, sir.'

'Umh. I'm sure they're a fine bunch of men, Number One, but we must keep up appearances. They look a scruffy lot to me. Most look as if they've not seen a razor or the barber for weeks. And the Coxswain's not setting an example.'

'Commander Smith never bothered much about show. He just wanted the fastest destroyer...'

'And so we shall be. The first to fire. The first to hit. *And* the smartest. It's easy to let things slip, but it's just as easy to have standards. Any man who sets foot on the bridge will be on a charge if he's not smartly dressed, clean shaven and with disciplined hair. The rest will soon get the message.'

A shudder of dismay ran through the wardroom at Steadfast's intransigent demand – the men weren't used to this. They worked hard and lived hard, as did the men in every convoy escort in winter. Their quarters were cold and wet, and reeked with the smell of oil, damp clothes and vomit. Hammocks could rarely be slung at sea and the men slept and dozed in any corner that might be safe from the lurching and rolling of the ship. The food was awful even when the galley stoves could be lit. As like as not, eating was a grab what grub you can business, when weather and duties permitted. For hours on end the men were at action stations, knowing that they were never more than a few miles from the enemy, a few minutes from a torpedo and a few yards from a mine.

'And you, Sub Lieutenant…?'

'Ross, sir. Thomas Ross. Just three months with the ship, sir. I was at the Admiralty at the start of the war – in Intelligence. They didn't want to let me go, but I kept on badgering. I reckon they thought a few months on a destroyer in the North Sea and I'd be back banging on the door at Admiralty House.'

'And will you?'

'No, sir. It's your job I want, not a desk in the dark recesses of Whitehall.'

'Well, I'd better watch out, then,' joked Steadfast.

'You want my job, too, Sub Lieutenant…?'

'Henry Paris, sir. Not on your life, sir. I'm strictly hostilities only. As soon as we've pushed Jerry back where he belongs I'll be back teaching Classics. I'll do my bit and that's all.'

'And the others, Number One?'

'The Engineer Lieutenant is Archibald Sherman – a career Navy man. Knows all there is to know about the machinery. Then there's Doctor Kendrick. He's RNVR like me so he'll be back in his practice in the Highlands as soon as this show's over. And Guns is Stanley Jackson – warrant officer with bags of experience. He won't let you down.'

Steadfast, touchy at the least hint of anything less than perfection, frowned at this description. 'I hope *no one* will let me down, RN, RNR or RNVR. Anything else I ought to know?'

'Well, there is Runaway Rattlesnake,' replied Gardiner.

'Who the hell is he?'

'The convoy commander, Vice Admiral Walter Rawlinson. He's the 'let's get home before tea' type. After a day or two, he'll have the convoy spread out like the tail of a comet. Finds himself a nice fast collier to lead the convoy and goads her master to put on steam.'

'So I suppose it's a case of 'watch out for the stragglers'.'

'That it is, sir, with a vengeance.'

'OK, let's get the Quartermaster to clear the lower deck. I'd like to have a talk with the men before dinner. And, Number One, have a word with the Coxswain about smartening up.'

Commander Steadfast went off to his cabin to check the bundle of paperwork that had been thrust into his hands with indecent haste an hour earlier. He had a lot to learn, both about the ship and the convoy. But he

16

didn't have much to learn about war. He may have seemed rather brusque and harsh to his officers, but he was no land-based Johnny talking from the comfort of a warm office with a nearby canteen serving a three course lunch. Steadfast was as blooded as the next officer.

***

'So that's the new captain. Know anything about him?' Asked Robert Elphick, a torpedo man.

'A bit. I've got a mate down in the office. Met 'im in the Crown and Anchor this afternoon. Says the new captain was Number One on the *South Riding* when she went down,' replied his station companion Norman Greenwood, 'nasty business, that was – only eleven survivors, they say.'

'His fault, do you think?'

'Hope not. Don't suppose he'd be here if it was. He's a survivor, though. Went to Narvik when the place was already half burnt down and the sky was thick with Heinkels. My mate says he just missed a DSC – he was going over the side to pull men out, pushing boats through burning water – that sort of thing.'

'Heroic type, eh? Not sure that's good news for us. I prefer the cautious type myself. Hang on, he's going to speak.'

'Men,' said Steadfast in a strong, clear voice, 'I'm very proud that the *Defiant* should be my first command. I know that Jerry's given you and her a tough time, but you've proved to be a credit to the Navy.'

'He's right there. We can match any ship any day,' muttered Elphick.

'I'm the new boy around here, but I'm not new to destroyers. She's the second I've served on, and I've been on a minesweeper. I've seen some tough times myself, so I can guess what we might be in for. We're Tilbury-bound tonight. The weather looks doubtful, which should keep Jerry out of the way. Pity, but we'll have our chance to get at him when the weather clears.'

'Bloody hell, does he want to be mangled into mincemeat and dumped in the sea? I hope he'll leave us out of it if he does,' griped Greenwood.

'And he says he knows about destroyers! Just wait until he's been up and down E-boat alley a few times. That'll shake him,' responded Elphick.

'Aye, E-boat alley will strike fear into *any* man,' replied his companion.

17

Chapter 3- Defiant Goes To Sea

Dinner in the wardroom that evening was a quiet affair at first. Under Smith the officers had enjoyed a hearty level of ribaldry and repartee, but in the presence of a new captain they awaited his lead.

But Steadfast preferred to listen while he sized up his men. He was far from impressed with Gardiner. RNVR was bad enough – but how could anyone think that weekend sailing in a dinghy was a preparation for war? And, on top of that, he was an actor! Inwardly, he exploded at the thought of a Sunday-sailor, would-be Hamlet, being Officer of the Watch when it came to dodging torpedoes. As for Ross, he seemed to be a plant from HQ. All 'When the First Sea Lord said...' and 'I think the First Lord would prefer...'. It was quite clear where *his* ambitions lay. And what a show-off with his Maserati Tipo 26B and his rosettes from this rally and cups from that. He wondered what Ross would do if he was stuck on the bridge when bombs were falling all around. Then there was young Paris, with the emphasis on 'young'. He may have sculled to victory on the Thames in the 1939 Oxford and Cambridge boat race, but one look at him suggested that was his limit. So juvenile in appearance and no hint of command in his face and manner. He seemed cowered by his colleagues round the table. And at dinner he had *three* times referred to Greek and Roman texts. At his age, mused Steadfast, I thought of only two things: the Navy and women, preferably unattached and in bed. No, not officer material in Steadfast's book. Guns and Lieutenant (E) sounded good types, though, – proud of their jobs and not too ambitious. He liked the way Guns kept emphasising the need for gunnery practice – a good practical type.

When the Chief Steward, Walter Peters, had finished clearing away dinner and disappeared to the galley, Steadfast passed round the port as a preliminary to exploring his fellow officers' views on convoy work.

'So, gentlemen, what makes a good convoy escort?'

Gardiner took the bait, mistakenly thinking that Steadfast was asking for advice.

'Well, sir, I would say your first job is to keep the convoy nice and tight, and to set an example by keeping close up ourselves. The really important thing is not to get distracted and go off chasing Jerry or herding in stragglers.'

'Sounds rather tame to me. Where's the Nelson flourish or the Beatty dash?'

'If you ask me, sir, they wouldn't have been much good at convoy work. All they had to do was fight the enemy – they didn't have to think of anyone else. In this sort of work, it's the commodore's convoy, not ours. We're the servant, not the master. We go at their speed, we follow their route, and we hope to arrive safe and sound all together.'

'Are you not keen on getting at Jerry, then, Number One?'

'I don't think that's what we're mainly here for, sir. We're here to protect. It's not our job to provoke big fights. Anyway, if we were to allow ourselves to be lured away from the convoy in swashbuckling adventures, the convoy would soon be set upon.'

'I'm with the captain on this,' interrupted Ross. 'It's our tradition to attack and not to let the enemy get away. Remember the Goeben and Breslau in the last war? How they ran rings round old Arky-Barky? There's an admiral who sat back and waited. We don't want to end up like he did, do we?'

'What happened to him?' asked Sherman.

'Exonerated and put on half-pay for the rest of the war,' replied Ross.

'You're very quiet, Paris,' said Steadfast.

'I'm not sure that I can add much, sir. I've only been in the Navy for two months. You've all known the Navy for years. But names like Goeben and Arky…?'

'Admiral Sir Archibald Berkeley Milne,' interjected Ross.

'Thank you, and Berkeley Milne, they mean nothing to me,' continued Paris.

'At least that's honest, Paris,' said Steadfast. 'If you want to learn, this is the ship to do it on. We're a fighting ship, and we'll happily teach you to be a fighting man.'

'Now, gentlemen, I've got a ship to get to know, so I'll leave you to continue the debate between yourselves.'

The wardroom fell silent, no one daring to speak until they were certain that Steadfast was safely back in his cabin.

'What was all that about?' asked Paris.

'It's about a raving nutter who wants to use this ship to re-fight the Battle of Trafalgar. He doesn't seem to care a damn about the convoy, all he wants is a good fight and plenty of mentions in despatches,' chimed a shocked Gardiner.

'Hang on a minute,' said Ross excitedly, 'he's talking about fighting, and that's what this ship is for. We're in the Navy, for God's sake. What else are we here to do?'

'To protect, as I said before,' responded Gardiner in an irritated voice. 'If we let that man turn us into some kind of freelance prize-seeking outfit, the convoy will be at the bottom in no time. Every decision we make, every action we take has to be for the convoy's sake. And as for our using our escort duty as a quick way to some flashy medals, well, words fail me!'

'I hope we're not going to quarrel for the rest of this convoy,' said Paris in a perplexed and anxious voice.

'There'll be no quarrel so long as we put the convoy first. Of course, we have to obey orders. Fine. But we should all do our best to keep the brakes on the captain, or he'll run us into serious trouble,' replied Gardiner.

'I hope you're not speaking for me,' said Ross, 'I think the Captain talks a lot of good sense.'

'Do you?' said Gardiner rising from his seat. 'Then Heaven help you.'

And with that Gardiner left the wardroom, slamming the door behind him. A bewildered Paris stared at an animated Ross. They'd all got on so well under Captain Smith. What had gone wrong?

**

The men's supper was quickly over. No one wished to linger as the hour of sailing approached. Steam had been up for some time now and the power line from the dockside long since withdrawn. Over the Tannoy came the call, 'Special sea duty men to their stations. Hands fall in for leaving harbour.'

Men made last checks on anything that could move. Hatches not in use were battened down. Portholes (or scuttles as they called them) were locked tight and their deadlights firmly sealed. On deck, cables were secured, boats and Carley floats were checked. Down below all the galley equipment not immediately needed was put away. The cable party took one last look at the anchor gear and the men made one final check on the blackout – a single chink of light at sea could mean the end of the ship.

At last the ship's two umbilical cords were let go: the shore telephone line was disconnected and the gangway withdrawn. The cable party forward waited for the order to raise the anchor. Then the motor stirred into life with its scraping, rasping noise. The long chains on the deck inched into motion. Link by link the cable was wrenched round the capstan, while two men hosed the muddy, weed-covered chain in the hawse pipe. Now clean, the chain tumbled into the locker, guided by another hand to ensure even packing. With a loud clang the anchor settled in the hawse pipe and the men rushed to secure the Blake slips. A loose anchor at sea was at least one hazard they could eliminate.

***

On the bridge Steadfast and Gardiner had watched the cable party as they waited for the ship to proceed.

'What's the latest forecast, sir?' asked Gardiner.

'Gales – westerlies,' replied Steadfast. 'It's going to be a bad night.'

'No need to worry, sir, this ship can take anything.'

'Not that kind of 'bad', Number One. Bad because we won't get any sport with the enemy. We'll hardly be able to find each other, let alone find Jerry.'

'Oh, I see, sir. I rather think I'll settle for the bad weather in preference to the E-boats.'

Defiant was now under way. One hundred-and-seventy men thought of their homes and wondered if they would ever see them again. Some had left wives and children. Some would return to find themselves fathers. Others to find they had been bereaved. Some, like Steadfast, had found a new love in their life and now suffered an anxious separation. All could not help thinking that they might not return. Some would be right.

Alone among all the souls on *Defiant*, Steadfast dreamed of action and glory. Out there was the enemy – *his* enemy – and *so* near. The Steadfasts had to seek and destroy. Nothing else would avenge the wrongs his family had suffered. Yet he suspected that, to a man, his colleagues would settle for just surviving the run to the Thames.

***

21

The *Defiant* proceeded slowly, first making her way through the mass of shipping in the harbour approaches and then finding her passage down the narrow waterway to the sea. In the darkness Steadfast eyed the twisted hulks of wrecks awaiting repair: masts leaning at every conceivable angle, bridges bent through ninety degrees, a bow missing here, a stern there. Each contorted skeleton in this graveyard was a ghastly reminder of the fate of those who ventured into the North Sea in war. He shivered as he recognised a particularly mangled ship. A good few years ago he had been a sub on her. Now he could barely make out the location of his old cabin amongst the twisted spars and crumpled steel.

'Boom ahead,' called a lookout. It swung open and *Defiant* slid through, a low black mass with her foaming wake churning the still harbour waters behind her. The boom closed and *Defiant* was alone on the dark sea.

The wind freshened as the ship approached more open waters and she rose and dipped as she met the first waves.

The lookouts peered into the darkness in search of the first harbour channel buoy, marking the route to the convoy channel, but Gardiner could navigate it backwards. Watch in hand, he was as alert as either of the lookouts, determined to make sure that the vital buoys were not missed.

'Fifteen minutes to the first buoy,' called Gardiner.

A short steep sea struck up the ship's weather side and the wind freshened, but visibility was good.

'Buoy on the port bow, sir!'

'Steer twenty degrees to starboard.'

'Twenty degrees it is, sir.'

Then came the last harbour channel buoy. Beyond was the open sea and the waiting convoy to the Firth of Forth and south to London.

Chapter 4 – Forming The Convoy

Defiant was quite early on station. As usual there were always one or two merchant men that turned up late. The convoy was supposed to move off at midnight but it could take hours to hustle the independent minded masters into order. How they resented being bossed around by the Navy! Tonight, though, the convoy was looking promising. By 11.00 pm it was steadily forming, with most of the thirty-five small coasters, tankers and miscellaneous freighters bobbing up and down in the lively sea. Their captains had all attended the commodore's briefing – a most incongruous affair since it was held in a peacetime ice cream parlour with enticing advertisements on the peeling walls for pre-war ices and sodas. The masters, in plain clothes, along with their Royal Navy signals ratings, had listened as the commodore gave them details of their pendant numbers, which ensured that they would enter and leave the convoy at the right ports. Most of them had no need of his basic lesson on identifying German warplanes and the dreaded E-boats. By late 1941 they were all too familiar with these. But the commodore knew his masters' weaknesses when he reminded them to keep closed up and to repeat back all the signals they received. He had great admiration for the Merchant Navy but the bloody-minded independence of its masters was another matter. Discipline was all in a convoy, but discipline meant nothing to them.

Defiant joined the second escort destroyer, HMS *Tremendous*, and the corvette HMS *Keswick* in rounding up the unhurried merchantmen. Up and down the lines they went, checking that each ship was in place: *Daffodil, Queen of the Tyne, Rosemary…* The commodore considered it vital that the ships took up the positions allocated by him: those ships going to the earlier ports had to be in the column nearest the coast and the first to turn at each port had to take the rearmost stations so that they could turn off without passing through the convoy. But Gardiner knew that it was all rather futile. Ordering the convoy by destination could result in the fastest ships being in the rear and the slowest in the van. Within a day they would all be huddled together in a bunched up scrum.

The other way around would result in the convoy getting longer by the day. Still, they had to follow the commodore's dispositions.

'*Moira*'s not here,' noted Steadfast.

'We can leave her for now, sir. We know her master well. Old Goodridge delights in teasing us – always leaves things to the last minute just to keep us on our toes.'

'If you say so. All sounds a bit slack to me.'

'By Navy standards, yes sir. But these aren't Navy men. They're stubborn men, masters in their own domain. No one tells them what to do, war or no war.'

'Lucky for them we're not like that.'

'Here she comes now, sir. Twenty-eight seconds to spare!'

The *Moira* passed *Defiant* close enough for Edward Goodridge to look Gardiner in the eye. Gardiner gave a shrug and a half smile of resigned acceptance of the master's wilful individualism. The two men had only met at the pre-convoy briefings but over the months Gardiner had come to admire the solid fortitude and long-suffering nature of masters such as Goodridge. They had a horrendous existence as they commanded worn out ships, badly maintained and lacking any modern equipment – many did not even have revolution counters or any means for the master to communicate with the engine room. They were badly paid and their onboard accommodation was not much better than a slum. For Gardiner, they were the forgotten heroes of the war at sea.

Midnight came and the convoy was still forming. Steadfast listened to the sound of the megaphoned voices as masters called to each other in search of their stations. 'Christ, can't they even take position?' he cried. Gardiner chose to ignore the impatience of his captain.

Finally the commodore signalled the convoy's departure, two hours late. Beside him on the bridge of the 2000 ton collier *Doncaster Races*, her master called, 'Half ahead,' and led off into the darkness. She passed to starboard of the first channel marker buoy – the last light in the dark sea until the next buoy five miles down the convoy route.

Slowly the thirty-five ships fell into line in their two columns a quarter of a mile apart, each vessel supposedly 400 yards behind the one in front, gradually gaining speed to reach the scheduled 7-knots. On the port side of the convoy lay *Defiant*, to starboard was *Tremendous*. At the rear was the corvette HMS *Keswick*, whose job was to hassle stragglers and pick up shipwrecked men from the murderous sea.

***

'How strange all this feels,' remarked Steadfast.

'What, sir?' responded Gardiner.

'Being trapped in a sea lane a few hundred yards wide in the dark. Out there to port is the northbound lane; out there to starboard are shoals and rocks. It was all so different on the Atlantic route – nothing to either side for thousands of miles.'

'Yes, that's why the commodore's so keen on station-keeping. Hardly a day passes without a collision, and groundings are common enough.'

'Well, I can't say I like it. Those masters don't know a thing about navigation – they just follow their noses. Gives me the creeps.'

'Not to worry, sir. Most of them have been up and down this coast for more years than you or I have been at sea. They're trained in the school of hard experience. They've as good a chance of getting through this trip as we have.'

'We'll see,' said a sceptical and contemptuous Steadfast.

For all his experience on the Atlantic route, Steadfast had never really got to know or respect the life of a master. He had missed the convoy briefing meeting that evening, so his experience of the merchant fleet was limited to the view from the bridge of the *South Riding*. Coming from a family with naval connections going back to before Trafalgar, he had a near religious respect for the ways of the Senior Service and nothing but condescension for the merchantmen, who did not know one end of a sextant from the other. As to the RNVR... He began to muse on how to ease Gardiner off into another ship.

***

Back on the bridge, staring into the darkness, Steadfast felt a sudden gust of wind and rain. Underneath him he sensed the ship's more lively movement. He knew from the strength and precipitousness of the blast that this was the first intimation of the forecast squall. But not even his year on the Atlantic had prepared him for the battle with the elements that was now to commence.

Down below, the ship was settling into the seemingly endless routines of convoy life. It was an endurance test for both the ship and the men. In a storm – and one was on the way that night – everything was wet. The bulkheads were wet, the deckheads dripped, the decks were often under water. Water came pouring down the ladders, settled in lockers and swilled around the men's feet. In the unheated messes all was cold and the only dry place was a man's hammock – but they were useless in a rough sea. At least, though, there were always the hot pipes in the boiler room for drying out soaking clothes and sodden sea boots.

Phillips came down the ladder into the petty officers' mess, his oilskins dripping into the puddles on the deck. As he eased off his sea boots he tipped them out and a fresh stream of salty water ran down the steeply sloping deck.

'You know what? Tonight I wouldn't mind a posting to a big ship.'

'You? You're not a big ship man. Officers everywhere. Routines like an Army parade ground,' responded Quartermaster Henry Cole.

'Aye, but we'd have a mess that didn't look and smell like a stinking canal.'

'So you would, but who'd give up this life for one of those floating hotels? This ship's a machine and you're part of it. We're all guns, depth charges and torpedoes and we're in the action night and day. You'd miss that.'

'Maybe I would, maybe I wouldn't, but some days I think I've had enough. Look at it. Nine months on this tin can with no more than a day or two of home leave. Month after month of twenty-four hour turnarounds. You get in, shattered, tired and fed up to your back teeth with the non-stop sailing, patrolling, docking, sailing...'

'Yes, yes. I get the message. But I bet you don't put in for a transfer when we dock next week.'

'*If* we dock. You're forgetting the new captain.'

But a man like Cole was not going to forget the new captain. Cole was another Great War veteran and knew how to size up both men and officers. Just as one 'dong' was enough to reveal the crack in a bell, so his first encounter with Steadfast had set Cole on edge. There was something not right; something most definitely not right for *Defiant*. There were officers that became part of the ship and officers who never belonged. Somehow he did not see Steadfast falling into the first category. Yet he and Steadfast would have to get along. He would be at the wheel whenever the going got tough and he and Steadfast needed to anticipate each other's thoughts when the bombs started dropping or the deadly torpedoes were streaking over the sea. But no man on the ship was less inhibited by Steadfast's arrival than Cole. An amateur boxer when young, his tough countenance, battered and reshaped by far too many punches and years of harsh exposure to sun, sea and wind, did not belie the interior man. He stood his ground, looked men and officers defiantly in the eye and knew his own mind. Rough in looks and rough in manners, he could handle the ship like a baby in a cradle, easing her into crowded docks, neatly placing her alongside an oiler or dodging 500 pound bombs plummeting from a hostile sky. Steadfast needed him more than he needed Steadfast.

***

Despite the signs of a rough night to come, Steadfast relaxed a little, now that the hazardous exit from port had been safely accomplished. He hadn't properly got to know his new ship and did not yet know which men he could most depend on. When the call to go to sea had come he was enjoying his first decent bit of leave of the war, staying at a friendly small hotel at Keswick. He had just met Virginia and after a few days of getting to know each other they had had a wonderful dinner and dance together. Next morning at 8.00 am a loud thumping on the bedroom door and the shout of 'Telegram, commander!' brought his idyll to an end. 'You are ordered to report with all despatch to…'. A frantic packing, a kiss, and he was gone.

Steadfast was actually rather disturbed by the emotions that Virginia had aroused in him. Until a week or two ago he had disparaged those officers who took up entanglements in times of conflict. There should be no distractions from the relentless waging of war at sea, no baggage left at home that could undermine the unremitting need to watch the sea, attend to the ship and drive the men on. Nor should his officers or his men see in him the least sign of any slackening in his work and his commitment. He despised himself for having succumbed to Virginia's spell – *she* was no one-night stand. Somehow he felt less in control of himself, which meant less in control of his ship and his wartime career.

He recalled his conversation of less than twenty four hours ago with Vice Admiral C G Ramsay of the Coast of Scotland Command, Rosyth:

'I hardly need to remind you, Commander, that being on an escort ship is like a marriage: she and the convoy are with you night and day, for better or worse… and there's a good deal of the 'worse'. Any family?'

'Not near enough to visit, sir.'

'Good. Better that way.'

Had he misled the admiral, or should he count Virginia as family? The truth was that she *was* near enough to visit – she worked at an Admiralty outpost in London.

'Pfft.' Steadfast mentally kicked himself for his reverie. It was time to get a grip on himself and the ship.

The bridge was familiar enough. He'd done two years on an old W-class destroyer, but this first command was a great step up. With the aid of the dim light of the chart table he surveyed his new home. There was the voice pipe to his sea cabin that would bring calls to him night and day – there would be no chance of any proper sleep until the convoy was safely home. There were the telephones for the engine room and the guns. The binnacles contained the magnetic compass and the gyrocompass repeater.

With the gathering storm not yet a serious problem Steadfast decided that it was safe to leave Ross alone on the bridge.

'Carry on, Sub Lieutenant. I'll be in my sea cabin,' said Steadfast.

Chapter 5 – A Storm To Remember

For some time both the officers and the men had been noticing the worsening weather. The ship seemed to rise and fall more. The easy motion of the first hour or two had given way to more sudden blasts of sea-soaked wind and the ship seemed heavier as she had to fight her way through the mounting waves. The occasional slamming gust of wind felt like a herald of worse to come.

'Weather report, sir.' Steadfast took the message sheet from Sparks.

'Doesn't look good. Force 10 westerly winds. Heavy rain. Will the convoy hold?' he asked Ross.

'Hope so, sir. They may not be Navy, but they've all seen the worst,' replied Ross.

'Even if they haven't, they will now. Prepare the ship for rough weather,' ordered Steadfast.

Men were piped to all corners of the ship as they scrambled to secure once more the *Defiant* against the coming onslaught. The wind was already sweeping across the ship from starboard to port. Men clung to stanchions, grabbed ropes and leant against the superstructure as they tried to stay upright on the slippery deck. Kneeling over hatches, they furiously screwed them down ever tighter. Others turned to the boats, checking all the lashings and adding extra gripes. Down in the galley, men were stowing away all stores and utensils except those needed for the all-essential hot cocoa. In the messes personal belongings were stuffed into lockers and floors were cleared. Back on deck, men were setting lifelines across the flats and by the torpedo and depth charge stations.

'Look at the men,' yelled Steadfast against wind 'they can barely move for fear of being blown overboard.' His remarks were seconded by the slam of a wall of water on the side of the bridge.

'Yes. Looks like we're in for it. At least the storm will keep Jerry away,' said Gardner, appearing on the bridge.

'There you go again. We want Jerry right here to give him the beating he deserves. That's the point of a convoy: to draw the enemy to our guns,' retorted Steadfast.

'Try telling that to the poor sods on those merchantmen. They never signed up for war. A good few are violently opposed to being forced into convoys. They hate the Admiralty and they're none too keen on us. We see ourselves as their saviours. Most of them see us as those bastards that force them to steam at the speed of the slowest. Have you ever talked with the masters, sir?'

'Can't say that I have.'

'Just try it, but not with your back to the wall. They'll rant about how you can't sail a merchant man at an arbitrary speed. The right speed depends on the cargo, the sea, the wind, and heaven knows what. Too fast and the sea will slam over the bows and smash the deck cargo to pieces. The wrong speed and the engine will vibrate like a cake-walk and shake itself to bits.'

'So, what's all this about?' quizzed a discomforted Steadfast.

'It's about remembering that the masters in the coastal convoys don't love us – they put up with us, that's all.'

'I don't give a damn for their opinions. We're here to fight a war and the sooner we can find Jerry, the sooner we can send him to the bottom.'

***

Within an hour the sea and wind had risen to an infernal crescendo. The ship no longer steamed through the water but was tossed like a scrap of paper scudding along a windy pavement. Out there in the blackness lay the convoy – by now scattered in every direction and probably making no headway at all. But the sea closed around *Defiant*, trapping her in a cauldron of swirling water. The winds roared, howled and screamed around the bridge. Ross battled to stay upright by shoving himself into the corners of the bridge. His face was stinging with the water smashing over him. To protect his eyes from the weight of water thundering down on him he held up a megaphone the wrong way round. It wasn't ideal, but at least he could see something that way.

The storm clawed and tugged at every element of the ship from the guardrails to the mast and rigging. Radio aerials were smashed from side to side. Lines crashed and whipped against metal and the boats rocked in their chocks as the wind sought to carry them away. When the great waves rose and rose to tower over the *Defiant* she seemed a mere pygmy. Then those same waves fell. Rivers of dark green water smashed into the superstructure with a noise like a dozen exploding shells. The ship staggered on, labouring to keep afloat. Now and again her stern would rise out of the water and her screws raced in the foaming wake. The chief's experienced hand speedily closed the throttle before the driveshaft smashed itself to pieces. Fear ran through the ship as every man closed in on himself. Every new crash of a wave on the side of the ship set each man shuddering. Every brief moment of calm, when the ship was momentarily at the peak or trough of a wave, caused hearts to stop and stomachs to tighten. The strength and wits of one-hundred-and-seventy men and the power of the ship's 19,000 shaft horse power engines were reduced to nothing by the infernal might of the sea. Men and ship were descending into a hell of unimagined proportions.

***

As Ross looked down from the bridge he could see the momentous torrents of water slamming over the fo'c'sle, tearing off everything that was not a part of the ship. Before his eyes he saw the guardrails twisted like a piece of creative origami.

The storm was now rising to its full power, driving the dark grey-green waves higher and higher. On the bridge Ross felt the *Defiant* rising up and up on a mounting wave. Then a moment of suspense. Thump. She plunged down from the heights before being swept up by the next mountain. He tottered, grabbed a railing and jammed himself into a corner. Less lucky was a leading seaman, who was washed off his feet and thrown against the side of the bridge. He struggled up, clearly in pain, clutching his side. More broken ribs, thought Ross. It was one of the great hazards of a storm. He sent the man below to see Kendrick. Ross was somewhat resentful that a man who barely knew one end of a ship from another should share his rank, but he knew that Kendrick was a first class doctor. His twenty years as a family physician in the Highlands had made him a perceptive diagnostician and a resourceful practitioner, who was used to working far from specialist facilities.

Now and again Ross caught a glimpse of the collier ahead – almost certainly way off station. Indeed, not a single ship would have the least idea of her position after the night's diabolical battering. *Defiant* and the collier ahead kept up a violent rhythmic performance. They plunged down and disappeared beneath the high sea, only to be born up again by the next rising wave. Up and down, up and down the two ships went, nose-diving through the seething mass of water. Way off on the starboard bow low grey smudges told him that the convoy was still there. All of it? Who could tell. It was pointless to try to count the ships in this weather.

Out on the deck not a man was in sight. The few at their stations huddled in the gun enclosures or in any corner that offered some protection from the torment.

Ross was used to the pitching. That was normal. But the yawing was more worrying. In the wheelhouse the helmsman was struggling to hold the course. Then came another swelling up of the wind, gust upon gust, each larger than its predecessor. Wham! The wheel was torn from the helmsman's hands as he was thrown across the wheelhouse. 'Nothing broken,' he yelled to the bridge – not that they could possibly have heard in the storm. He staggered back to the wheel.

The loneliness and the horrors of the bridge were broken by a voice from the ladder.

'Anyone for cocoa?' It was Peters.

'Yes. And lots of it,' shouted back Ross.

Peters, arms out to help him balance, teetered over to the ladder and disappeared. Down in the galley he found a cook desperately restraining pots and jugs on the galley stove as the ship rolled and pitched.

'A jug for the bridge,' he called.

Bracing his heavy body in the angle between the stove and the doorway, the cook filled a jug from the cauldron and passed it to Peters. Peters tucked the jug under one arm, four cups dangling from his fingers. As he made his slithery, lurching way back to the ladder, the ship threw him from one wall of the corridor to the other. Each time that he was thrown, he turned to fall backwards onto the oncoming wall, holding the precious cocoa outwards. At the foot of the ladder he steadied himself. Feet well apart, he waited for the brief pause between the ship shooting upwards and the following plunge down. He grabbed the ladder rail with his left hand, put one foot on the bottom rung and pulled himself up. Two feet on. Pause. Back against the other rail. Another foot. Pull. Pause. Slowly he dragged himself up with the cocoa swaying at his side and the sea trying to wrench him from the ladder. But Peters was no novice. He reached the top of the ladder, took the deepest breath he could ever imagine and yelled over the roar of the wind, the thunder of the waves and the creaking of the ship, 'Cocoa!' A hand took the jug from him and he pulled himself up onto the bridge.

Elphick and Greenwood didn't merit a steward to wait on them. Now two hours into their watch at the torpedo tubes, cold and oozing water like two newly-dipped sponges, Elphick looked at his colleague.

'Time for cocoa. You or me?'

'Toss for it.'

Greenwood flipped a penny and Elphick called 'Tails.'

'Off you go,' said Greenwood.

Elphick heaved himself off the deck where they were both sitting. Grabbing a stanchion he stood uneasily for a moment as his body adjusted to the lurching movements of the ship. There was no hope of walking to the ladder. All he could do was to fling himself from stanchion to stanchion, from rope to rope. As he reached the ladder a towering wave of black water and white foam crashed over him, flooding down the companion way. Elphick followed it down and waded to the galley.

'Rough up top?' asked the cook.

'Bloody tornado, I'd say. It beats me why we're out there in this weather. We'd never be able to stand up and fire the torpedoes.'

'Never trust Jerry.'

'Anyway, we're up there, so we need something to warm us.'

Swaying and rolling, the cook somehow filled a jug without spilling a drop, and handed it to Elphick.

'This'll make you forget the gale.'

'Some hope,' replied Elphick.

Clutching, the cocoa jug and cups he fought his way back to his station, much as Peters had done to the bridge.

'Didn't think I'd see you again,' joked Greenwood.

They poured out the cocoa – two full cups each – and momentarily enjoyed its sweet warmth. Then they settled back into their silent waiting, huddled in their sou'westers, oilskins and sea boots. From time to time they shuffled to ease their numbed bodies, while they stared out over the rain and mist-strewn sea.

Chapter 6 – Disaster Aft

Back on the bridge, Ross was inwardly confident that he could handle *Defiant* in the pitch-black night, despite the storm. He took out his glasses and surveyed the scene. On the starboard bow was, he hoped, the *Mermaid*. At times she was just visible as a hint of a black lump. At other times Ross could make out nothing. After an hour or so he no longer trusted his eyes. Sometimes he was sure that he had found *Mermaid* dead ahead, then she disappeared and he found her well to starboard. Every now and again he would call out to the lookouts, never letting on that he had next to no idea of what was ahead.

'Anything to report?'

'Mermaid still ahead,' replied the starboard lookout.

'Nothing to this side, sir,' came the voice from the port lookout.

It's easy for them, thought Ross. They changed watch every half-hour. But he might not have trusted them so much had he thought of the time needed for a man's eyes to adjust to the darkness when he came up from below. In the submarines a man lay in total darkness for fifteen minutes before going on watch at the periscope. No such precautions were taken on *Defiant*. So when a new watch came on Ross's faith in the men was on the optimistic side.

The watch changeover coincided with the storm reaching a fresh crescendo. As the men of the new watch came up onto the bridge, the old watch was near enough washed away down the ladder. Mountainous waves fell on the bridge, forcing Ross to grab any rail or handhold that he could in order to stay upright. Briefly the bridge deck would show beneath the men's feet, but almost immediately a new wave left them paddling in inches of water. As the men looked out to sea they had to repeatedly turn their backs to the oncoming waves. Their lookout role was as much for themselves as for the ship.

Ross had been on watch for three hours. Three hours of anxiety. Three hours of trying to make sense of the senseless black. And three hours of an exhausting personal battle with waves and wind. When not clinging for his life as the sea cascaded over him, he was desperately grasping on rails, binnacles and seats to counteract the pitching and rolling of the ship. Never for a moment did the ship seem to be horizontal. His legs ached from the endless effort of buttressing his body against the motion. His arms felt as if they were being tugged from their sockets as the sea strove to sweep him from the bridge into the black depths below. And every corner of his body was dulled with cold. He felt as if the numbing cold of the wintry sea had entered the deepest parts of his being.

In short, Ross was paying more attention to himself than to the wanderings of the convoy and the course of the *Defiant*. He was brought rapidly back to reality by a cry from one of the lookouts.

'Collier on starboard bow, sir!'

'Where? I can't see anything.'

'There, sir, there!'

Out of the mist, rain and spray a dark grey mass appeared, heading straight for *Defiant*'s stern.

'Hard to port,' he yelled into the wheelhouse voice-pipe.

'She's coming at us, sir!'

'Stop the port engine!'

In terror Ross glanced at the compass. Would *Defiant* respond? Would the needle never move? The grey mass was gaining on them. Two thousand tons of steel was heading for *Defiant*'s bow. One degree. Moving at last. Two degrees... three... four.

'Starboard engine full ahead!'

Suddenly Ross realised that the terror-struck lookouts were watching him.

'Get to your posts! Get to your posts!'

By now the lurching of the *Defiant* had awakened the whole ship. Men were thrown from where they slept. The few remaining loose items in the ship went skidding across the decks and tables. In his sea cabin the pad on which Steadfast was writing was wrenched from his hand and his pen fell to the deck.

'What's happening, Ross?' cried Steadfast as he bounded onto the bridge.

But he hardly needed to ask. There was the collier on the starboard bow. Under his feet Steadfast felt the rapidly turning *Defiant*, heeling as she sought to avoid collision.

Still turning, *Defiant* seemed to heel ever nearer into the raging sea on her port side as she gained speed.

'We'll make it, sir,' cried Ross.

All eyes were now on *Defiant*'s bow – the latest target of the approaching collier. The collier's high bow now towered over *Defiant* as the distance between the two ships shortened. Thirty yards... *Defiant* kept turning... twenty... ten... *Defiant*'s swinging stern now seemed to rush towards the collier's prow. Ross closed his eyes. Crash!

***

All on the bridge felt the terrifying crunch as the two ships collided. It was perhaps a matter of seconds but it felt like hours as the collier ground into *Defiant*, sheering chunks off her as she buried into the ship's side. The sound of tearing, grinding metal could clearly be heard above the howling gale. Every man froze as he waited for some final cataclysmic injury to the ship. Then *Defiant* swung clear of her assailant. The collier passed ahead of *Defiant* and disappeared into the swirling mass of sea and darkness.

There was no sudden list. No great rush of water into the hold. *Defiant* was still in one piece.

'Get her back on course, Sub Lieutenant. At this rate we'll lose sight of the convoy in minutes,' said Steadfast in a calm voice.

Steadfast may have been cool and in control, but Ross's legs had turned to jelly and his heart was pounding like an engine on a Blue Ribbon run. Despite the cold of the sodden ship, a rush of sweaty heat rushed through his body. Gripped by a terror which was tempered by his relief that the ship was still afloat, he came near to passing out. A barked, 'Sub Lieutenant!' from Steadfast brought him back to his senses.

'Half ahead port,' said Ross to the engine room.

'Course one-three-five.'

'Coxswain, find Mr Beverton and tell him to take some men aft to check the damage.'

Phillips handed the wheel to Able Seaman Hancock and disappeared down the ladder to find Beverton.

Meanwhile, Steadfast mulled over what to do about Ross. By rights he ought to come down hard on him, yet Ross was the man from the Admiralty and a career sailor. What a bunch, he thought. Lothario Gardiner, who seemed to lack any aggressive streak, and Paris, whose head was back in the ancient world. Young Beverton showed promise, but it was early days with him. The one hopeful amongst them was Ross. No, he muttered, 'I'm going to need him before this convoy gets home.' And, of course, as an Admiralty man, Ross could prove useful back on land. Better to help him along and leave the others to muddle through.

***

While Steadfast was plotting how best to advance his career, Phillips, who had no desire at all to be promoted, had rushed off to find Beverton. He ran and slid down the ladder and burst into the wardroom, already panting from the strain of such unaccustomed rush on his ample and ageing frame.

James Beverton, almost a schoolboy, was the midshipman. His father had been a flotilla commander in the First World War and had stayed in the Navy until his retirement in 1935 as a rear admiral. For as long as Beverton could remember, dinner table talk at home had been about the Navy and the Great War. His childhood years had been filled with naval yarns told in the library in winter, and the same yarns repeated on the terrace and lawns in the summer. When no one was in the house he would sneak upstairs and try on his father's cap in front of the tall mirror on the landing. Never for a moment had he thought of any career other than the Navy. Now, just two months out of the Royal Naval College at Dartmouth, he saw himself at the start of a great naval career. His ambition was writ large in his deportment and manner. He strutted rather than walked, posed rather than stood, and commanded with the authority of a young man who saw the Navy as his birthright.

When Phillips found Beverton he was reading a sailing magazine. 'How does he do it?' Phillips asked himself. 'This storm's half-killing most of the men and there he sits, as happy as sandboy. He's got guts that young lad.'

'Captain wants to know the damage aft pronto. You're to take a party and report ASAP.'

'Damage?'

'Didn't you feel the collision? Bumped by a stray collier we were. Maybe a scratch. Maybe worse.'

'No, I think I must have been carried away by this article. It's about...'

'Doesn't matter now, what it's about, sir. It's an emergency up top.'

'Right,' replied Beverton, excited at the sound of the word 'emergency'. He leapt up and shoved his large feet into his sea boots.

As soon as Beverton appeared in the mess he saw a mass of anxious faces betraying their concern about the horrendous tearing and scraping sounds that they had just heard, even if he had not. But Beverton avoided their gaze and quickly picked out three men whom he could trust for the perilous task ahead.

'Johnson, Higgins, Roberts: up double quick. We're damaged aft.'

Beverton had picked his men with care. The weightlifting Able Seaman Johnson, who was worth two men in terms of muscle; the ever-willing Ordinary Seaman Higgins; and the quick-thinking Signalman Roberts. They were a good combination, and not one of them would shrink from a dangerous trip down the storm-swept deck. All were strong men, as the tug-of-war match photo in the mess testified.

There was a rush of putting cold feet into already damp sea boots, thrusting arms and legs into stiff oilskins and ramming sou'westers down onto heads. As the party reached the ladder they were greeted by a cascade of water from a massive wave which had just struck the ship. They paused a moment and then rushed up in the hope of beating the next onslaught.

On deck Beverton, Johnson, Higgins, and Roberts attached themselves to cold, dripping lifelines and began to make their way aft along the narrow deck between the sea and the ship's superstructure. The violently rolling ship flung them now against the superstructure, now against the guardrail. At times the roll touched thirty degrees. They strained every muscle to cling to the lifeline and the stanchions, their boots slithering on the foaming deck. The huge sea towered over them and crashed down as if determined to tear them from the vessel. Beverton was leading the file of bedraggled men when he suddenly stopped. He put up a hand to signal halt and then pointed to the edge of the ship. Shouting was no good in this storm, but the men soon got his message: the last twenty feet of guardrail had been torn away in the collision. A seaman lay sprawled on the deck, apparently motionless. Ross edged forward a few feet more in an attempt to reach the sailor. He stopped and waved a frantic 'Back! Back!' to the men behind him.

Swaying in the wind and slipping on the greasy deck, Beverton slowly turned round and inched his way back to his men. Above the thunder of the wind he yelled 'There's a man on the deck and the lifeline's gone.' They were still twenty feet from the injured man. Twenty feet of slippery deck, washed over by crashing wave after crashing wave.

Beverton pushed his men under the mean shelter of the rear gun.

'Higgins: get thirty feet of cable and a line for each man. Johnson and Roberts, wait here with me.'

Higgins staggered off to a locker, swaying and tottering, stopping at intervals to grab a railing or a stray handhold. Every few paces he had to wedge himself tight and grip whatever was at hand as yet another wave crashed over him. When he reached the cable locker, his cold hands fumbled at the catch. The lid sprung open and Higgins pulled out a cable and some lines. Ramming himself into a corner he passed the coiled lines and cable over his head, leaving him looking like the Michelin man. His hands now free, he prepared for the death-defying walk back to the rescue party.

'Well done, Higgins,' said Beverton, as Higgins rejoined the party. Beverton lifted the dripping cable from over Higgins's head.

'First, the easy bit,' he continued, 'Johnson: secure the cable to that ring-bolt.'

With his cold, wet hands, Johnson wrestled with the stiff cable, passing its sodden dripping mass through the ring-bolt and securing it with a buntline hitch.

'Cable's secure, sir,' yelled Higgins.

'Now comes the tricky bit,' said Beverton. 'I'm going to tie myself to the cable end and take it across the deck.'

Beverton attached his lifeline to the cable. Then he took a second line, tied it around himself and handed the end to Roberts.'

'Roberts: you hold tight to this in case things get sticky.'

'Aye, aye, sir.'

'Johnson, Higgins: you look after the cable.'

'Sir.'

Beverton waited for the next big wave to pass for a moment when the ship was reasonably level. Then, lying down flat on the deck, he began to crawl across towards the injured man. He grabbed at the least projection that he could find in order to gain a handhold, pulling the cable end behind him. Johnson and Higgins took up the slack at the other end.

Beverton had only gone a few feet when the next big wave smashed over him. He disappeared under the flood of water falling back into the sea from the heavily sloping deck. Then a crumpled, sodden hump reappeared. Beverton was still there.

After five minutes or so Beverton had got about fifteen feet down the deck. Each foot won was more perilous than the last, as the lengthening cable gained more and more play.

It was Higgins who saw it first. A monster wave. He shouted to Beverton, but the midshipman could hear nothing and, flat on the deck, had no view of the sea. 'It'll do for him,' shouted Higgins.

The wave – tons and tons of foaming, thundering water – plunged down as if determined on tearing the ship apart. The deck vanished before the eyes of the men. And they waited. Would the water never fall back into the sea? Then it did.

There was Beverton, clinging to a jagged remnant of the ripped off guardrail. A few moments later the ship was momentarily almost righted. Beverton seized the opportunity to haul himself over to the injured man. He was lying prostrate with one leg at an unnatural angle, a huge bleeding gash in his forehead and unconscious, and was clearly in a bad way. Beverton fumbled at his line, trying to work out how to attach it to the seaman, but he could find no means of getting the rope round the deadweight. As he clung to the seaman, wave after wave came thundering down onto them, throwing the unnaturally coupled men from one side of the deck to the other.

Beverton abandoned his attempt to secure the man. His only hope was to hold him tight. Riskily putting one hand into the air, he waved a 'pull me' signal to Higgins and then hastily regained his hold on the unconscious seaman.

'He's coming back! Heave, lads!'

Higgins, Roberts and Johnson pulled like they had never done before. With two men on the rope, the rolling deck and the thundering waves they felt they were in battle with the inferno itself. Inch by inch the deadweight came towards them. From time to time Beverton and the seaman disappeared under cascades of dark water. But each time, as the foaming mass fell back into the sea, their precious load reappeared.

And then came the greatest wave of all. They could see it coming like a towering juggernaut, high about the ship. The white-crested top was beginning to curl as the terrifying mass of water careered towards the deck. For a moment it seemed to hang, a threatening, raging mass. Then down it came, tearing, roaring, thundering until it exploded with a crash that shook the ship.

Higgins and his men had closed their eyes and recoiled in horror from the cataclysmic force. Each thought his last moment had come – and perhaps the ship's last moment too. So when they found themselves unharmed and the angrily crashing wave falling back into the sea they felt like condemned men on the scaffold hearing a prison officer reading out their reprieve. But when they looked aft, the deck was bare, with the cable now dangling over the side of the ship.

The men on the cable had felt the weight of the fall of Beverton and the injured seaman, but despite the heavy jerk, they had not lost their hold.

Roberts shouted 'Pull! Pull! Pull!'

They pulled. Nothing.

'Cable's caught,' yelled Roberts.

'I'll go down the line and take a look,' roared Higgins.

With his lifeline attached to Beverton's cable, Higgins crawled down the deck, feeling the cable inch by inch. The sea washed over him, the ship's roll pitched him first one way and then the other, but he held the cable with a vice-like grip and dug the toes of his boots into the deck.

Inch by inch he went. Then his left hand touched something: the stub of a ripped-off stanchion, with Beverton's line firmly wrapped around it. Firmly indeed. The line was taut as a bow string at the Battle of Agincourt. There were two men hanging on one end and Roberts and Johnson pulling on the other. Grabbing the line firmly with his right hand, Higgins tried to pull the rope up off the top of the stanchion stub. Not a hope, he thought. Then he remembered his pocket knife. It was in his right pocket, but his right hand was gripping the cable, which was all there was between staying on deck and joining Beverton. He passed his left hand under his body and tried to turn it to reach down into the pocket. The wet and twisted pocket had become a sealed-off pouch. Slowly, a tug at a time, Higgins pulled at the pocket to turn it inside out. Roberts and Johnson watched fearfully as the seconds ticked by. Every moment counted if they were to get Beverton back alive. And then, with one final jerk, Higgins's pocket plopped out and surrendered the knife. With the knife closed, he eased one end of its body under the rope and tried to lever it up off the stump. Still nothing. By now near the end of his strength, he tried one last time. The knife shot out of his hand and flew into the sea as the rope leapt off the stanchion. For a brief moment Beverton had been lifted up by a wave and his weight relieved from the line.

Johnson and Higgins felt the change in the line's tension and suddenly realised that it was moving.

'Bloody good job there's two us – we've got three of them on the line now!' said Roberts.

First to come in was Higgins, wetter than ever and with a lacerated left hand, but otherwise able-bodied. He joined the others on the line and the three men began to pull. Their hands were numb with cold, the line both rough to the skin, yet slippery from the drenching rain and sea. Their boots slipped on the deck as the ship rolled from side to side. But their pulling had no result. Was Beverton caught on something? There was no way of telling. All they could do was to tug, and tug they did. Slowly the rope came in, inch by inch.

'We're winning,' yelled Roberts against the wind.

'But where the 'eck's Beverton?' shouted Johnson.

'There!' cried Higgins.

A black, lifeless mass was just showing above the shattered gunwale. The men summoned up almost their last strength to pull Beverton up over the edge until he was sprawled motionless on the deck. The final ten feet or so seemed easy after the titanic efforts of the last few minutes. Soon Beverton lay at the feet of the three seamen. The injured seaman was gone.

'Is he dead?' asked Johnson.

'Don't know,' replied Higgins, 'Better get some help.'

Roberts re-attached himself to the main lifeline and fought his way back to the bridge.

'Beverton went overboard, sir. We've got him back, but looks like 'e's done for. There's a man overboard as well.'

'Get Mr Beverton below to the wardroom,' ordered Steadfast.

'Ross, get the doc to the wardroom double-quick.'

'And the man overboard?'

'There's nothing we can do for him in this storm. No one could survive it.'

It took five minutes for the men to drag the motionless Beverton along the pitching deck and down the ladder. They heaved the insensible, dripping mass up onto the wardroom table. Dr Kendrick stooped over him and began his examination.

'His pulse is gone,' he quietly reported.

Chapter 7 – The End of a Hard Night

The doctor tore off Beverton's sodden clothes and put the heel of his right hand on the midshipman's chest with his fingers over the heart and began rhythmically compressing it. Thirty compressions. Then a slow breath into Beverton's mouth – too fast and the air would go into the stomach. Beverton's chest rose slightly. Then a second breath. And back to the pumping. Kendrick must have known that the situation was desperate but no one could tell from his calm, professional actions. He seemed in control.

Phillips – who ought to have been back on other duties – stood helplessly watching, as did Johnson, Higgins and Roberts. Each minute seemed like an hour, yet Kendrick kept on. Every so often he stopped and checked for signs of life. The fifth check. Dr Kendrick felt Beverton's neck. He turned to his audience:

'He's going to make it, lads. Ask Gibbs to come and we'll get him warmed up and put to bed.'

Looking after Beverton would be good experience for Gibbs, thought Kendrick. As a new sick berth attendant, Gibbs was rather lacking in practical experience. He had left school just a few months ago and the only certificate that he had was from the St John's Ambulance. Naturally he was sent for training as a naval sick berth attendant. It was now just two weeks since he completed his 10-week emergency training course. Beverton would be his first real patient at sea.

***

When Gardiner took over on the bridge, Steadfast dozed lightly in his sea cabin for a couple of hours as the storm continued to rage. He needed to rest, but his mind would not let him. How far he had come in just twelve months. It was the man overboard that set him thinking. He remembered the first time that Lieutenant Commander Thomas Lomax had ordered South Riding to steam on, leaving screaming, shouting, bobbing heads in the Atlantic. He recalled with shame how he had remonstrated with Lomax – he had come very near to using the word 'murderer'. Lomax had given him a sharp lecture on the need for a captain to suppress his personal feelings and think of his higher duties. Steadfast had never told a soul about his quarrel with Lomax, and sincerely hoped that Lomax too had kept quiet. Now *he* had ordered his own ship to steam on, leaving a man to his fate. He was a harder, tougher commander now.

***

During the following day the storm gradually abated and a sense of calm and normality returned to *Defiant*. The storm damage to the ship was largely superficial so the officers and men instinctively fell back into the routines of the convoy. The still heavy sea below and the dense cloud above held the enemy at bay. The convoy kept up a steady 7-knots through a wild sea. Steadfast looked forward to having a chance to get at the Germans. Meanwhile, Gardiner brooded on the wild commander he was now serving. In all those years in the RNVR he had always seen the Navy as the first and last defender of Britain's liberty. Never had he seen it as an aggressive force – after all, you can't conquer other countries with a Navy – that was a job for an army. Now confronted with an aggressive commander he found himself unsettled and anxious. Who was right – him or Steadfast?

Paris was also reflecting on the events of that night. He had never imagined a storm such as this one, nor realised how difficult it was to navigate a ship at night in a storm. And when he saw the lifeless young Beverton being carried into the wardroom, the full horrors of the power of the sea showed him a new side to naval life. He had often wondered how he would face up to an air or torpedo attack. Now he had found a new enemy: the sea itself. Paris tried to catch a bit of sleep but, riddled with self-doubt, he was not at ease with himself.

Surprisingly, the one man who had come through that first terrible night with optimistic confidence was Ross. Despite the collision, he was exhilarated by the way that he had handled the ship after the collision and his intrepid watch on the bridge in the storm. His actions, he thought, had been in full naval tradition: bold, resolute and, as he now erroneously recalled, fearless.

So, as the second night fell, Steadfast and Ross felt ready for anything that Jerry or the sea could throw at them. But Paris and Gardiner feared they were faltering after just one day of this horrendous convoy. What, wondered the two men, could possibly come next?

Chapter 8 – Steadfast Is Deceived

The answer came that night. By 11.00 pm the weather was thick, the cloud low and dense. All that Steadfast could see from the bridge was an empty blackness. Out there, on station he hoped, were the sluggish colliers and the trudging tramps. The only sign of life on the *Defiant* was the glow of the binnacle light and the low rumbling of the engines below. Perhaps tonight will be a dull one, he thought, broken only by cocoa deliveries and watch changes. But there was still the risk of E-boats, and the men were jittery. The boats favoured a winter's night, and the light mist was ideal for their surprise attacks. An E-boat commander knew the tides and currents inside out. And the boats' 40-knots against the convoy's seven or so gave them near impunity from capture. Steadfast recalled that in September 1940 Heinz Birnbacher's flotilla had sunk four coasters in a single convoy. The boats would be out there somewhere, tied up to the British channel buoys to await the moment of attack. Steadfast relished the opportunity to do battle with them. Even better if Korvettenkapitän Wendorff was out there leading his flotilla.

The commander looked at his watch: midnight – the E-boat's habitual hour of attack. He mused on the futility of politicians' attempts to limit war. These boats were only here because of the Versailles Treaty. That treaty had restricted German warship building, but had left them free to develop small craft. When tonight's first torpedo came, it would be a present from Versailles, delivered by one of the most deadly war vessels ever invented. Their round wooden hulls kept them stable in the roughest seas and they could pass over magnetic minefields with impunity. As for their famed speed, their three Daimler-Benz diesel engines delivered 6000 horse power. That speed was further enhanced by their twin Lürssen rudders aside the main rudder, which kept their wake low. Although they had 20 mm cannons, the real killing power of these boats was in their two torpedo tubes and the four torpedoes that they carried. But they had to fire two torpedoes at a time – one port and the other starboard. (A single torpedo launch would set the E-boat spinning round.) So that gave each boat just two chances of a hit before having to flee. Or two chances before Steadfast could attack without reply.

One more thing worried Steadfast: the British motor launch ML145. He shuddered as he remembered his near sinking of one on his last ship. She was a long way off, in rain and mist – just a grey and white blur. They had had no notice of British launches in the area so he confirmed the order to fire. They must have fired a couple of hundred rounds before a lookout shouted 'She's one of ours.' Had the gunners' aim been better, he would have been up before a Court Martial. 'No mistakes tonight,' he said to himself.

'Number One, see how Gervass is getting on,' ordered Steadfast.

Gardiner went off to the radio room, where Gervass Vanderloop, the Headache operator, his headphones pressed to his ears, was hunched over his receiver, tweaking one knob after another. Gervass had been at his post for several hours, his radio tuned to the carrier wave frequency of the E-boat walkie-talkie radios. Those Germans were great chatterers, even when on a raid. And when they weren't talking they left their radios on so that their tell-tale carrier unwittingly betrayed their presence to the British.

'Anything up tonight, Gervass?' asked Gardiner.

'Not sure. A few carrier waves; some talk about weather. But the signals are weak. I don't think they're close.'

'Maybe they're still looking for us. Keep listening. And report to the bridge every fifteen minutes.'

Gardiner returned to the bridge.

'Well?' asked Steadfast.

'Maybe, maybe not. Gervass says the signals are weak.'

'It doesn't make sense. Jerry must know where we are – more or less. OK, maybe the E-boats are still searching, but they can't be far away.'

Back in the radio cabin, Gervass heard some new voices. His two years in Germany as a sales representative for a Dutch food processing machinery manufacturer had honed his listening skills to perfection:

'Udo, here. Are you there Friedrich?'

'Friedrich here.'

'We are at the buoy three miles ahead of the convoy. Where are you?'

'We are at the next buoy ahead.'

'Come here – not too quickly – avoid any noise. Attack at 0015.'

Gervass called the bridge: 'E-boats ahead – they're rendezvousing at the next channel buoy.'

'Bosun: pipe action stations.'

A press of a button and the clanging alarm rang through the ship from stem to stern. Lumps uncurled from under blankets; oilskins and coats bounced into life. No time for stretching and yawning. Feet were shoved into boots, sweaters rammed over heads. Clutching their coats and oilskins, men tore down corridors, through doors, up ladders, across flats to arrive at their stations. They ran like automatons, no sound but thundering feet and clanking doors. Within a minute or two the 4-inch, 2-pound Oerlikon guns were manned, as were the two torpedo tubes and the depth charge throwers.

Defiant was now ready to see off all comers. Her aldis lamp flickered a warning up and down the convoy and ships began to zigzag in the darkness.

At exactly fifteen minutes past midnight Steadfast saw rockets in the night sky a few miles behind *Defiant*'s position.

'Rockets at starboard 120,' called a lookout.

'Starboard 120, helmsman,' ordered Steadfast.

'Meet her.'

'Are you sure they'll be an E-boat when we get there, sir?'

'Of course. What do you mean?'

'Looks a bit suspicious to me, sir. Just some rockets and no other action. They haven't fired a single shot since then.'

'Not trying to avoid action are you, Number One?'

'No, sir. I just don't think we're going to find Jerry anywhere near those rockets.'

Gardiner was just about to explain to Steadfast that the Germans were a bit more subtle than Steadfast was, when they reached the area where the rockets had been seen.

'All quiet here, sir,' remarked Gardiner.

'Thank you, Number One, I can see that.'

Steadfast had fallen for the E-boat commanders' trick of setting off rockets to draw the escort to the wrong side of the convoy. Gardiner had been sure of this from the start, but he knew that Steadfast would not listen to an RNVR man. He had to learn for himself the wiles of the enemy.

'Course one-eight-oh. Full ahead, chief,' Steadfast quietly ordered, hiding his humiliation.

Chapter 9 – Steadfast's Triumph

Defiant had returned to moving with the convoy when a collier on the east side signalled, 'We are under attack by E-boats'. Almost simultaneously several convoy ships opened fire.

'We've been had, sir,' said Gardiner, secretly triumphant at Steadfast's misjudgement. 'The rockets were a decoy to draw us away from the main attack.'

'But we couldn't have known,' retorted Steadfast, unwilling to be included under 'we'.

'Well what else do you call it when we've been lured to the wrong side of the convoy?' retorted Gardiner, annoyed that his commander had taken no notice of his earlier hints.

If Steadfast noticed the tetchiness of his Number One, he didn't show it as he calmly ordered, 'Course oh-nine-oh, Quartermaster. Full ahead, Chief.'

Defiant was now racing to the other side of the convoy, which was lit up like a *son et lumière* display by the gun flashes, star shell and a flaming ship. She tore through the slowly zigzagging convoy, the spray from her bow shimmering under the star shell above, her wake angrily gushing out behind her. As she neared the attack zone, Steadfast could see two colliers listing, one of which was on fire. Boats and Carley floats were in the water.

Now Steadfast could see just how he had been deceived. The presence of the bulk of the E-boat flotilla was clear from the naval gunners on the merchant ships firing away in an easterly direction. No doubt about it: the E-boats were still there – still ready to launch more deadly torpedoes.

As *Defiant* reached the line of the ships under attack, Steadfast gave the order to slow engines.

'Fire at will,' he called.

The gunners scanned the sea for any sign of a craft – they couldn't rely on the director now since there could be half a dozen small targets within range. Tired eyes gazed across the lively dark sea. Now the sea was dimly lit by the flickering light of the burning collier. Now star shells illuminated the scene with the ghostly light of a macabre stage set. The colliers seemed too small to be hit, yet the weary gunners were searching for something far smaller. There was not a seaman on *Defiant* whose life was not at that moment in trepidation. All but the newest recruits had seen enough E-boat attacks to know the routine by heart: an explosion in the dark, a rocket flare from the stricken ship, the grinding, whining roar of the escaping E-boat and then the faint cries of drowning men coming out of the darkness. No man ever got used to these terrifying night hours. Many a man broke under the strain.

Up in the radio cabin Gervass could hear several E-boat commanders shrieking out orders to attack particular vessels, but it was hard to make sense of their exchanges since he could not know which ships the Germans were referring to.

The first sign that *Defiant* had of the continued presence of the E-boats was a collier turning away from an approaching torpedo. Steadfast could see her rapid manoeuvring as her naval gunners furiously pumped 4-inch shells into the dark sea. Suddenly the roar of the E-boat's powerful engines was gone. Had it been hit? Or had it cut its motors to lie idle before the next attack?

But the boat – or perhaps a different one – had another collier in its sights. The first that its master knew was when he heard a roar like the sound of a whining circular saw slicing through a tough piece of wood. A lookout cried, 'Torpedoes' and the master saw the shimmering phosphorescent streaks in the water coming straight for his ship. They were fast – perhaps 25-knots. He gave the order to turn but before the ship had begun to respond she was rocked by the smash of a torpedo into her stern. A plume of water towered over the ship, flames shot out from under the ripped open deck. And there was no sign of the attacker other than the departing roar of engines.

When *Defiant* reached the collier, a spine-chilling silence had descended on the ship, broken only by the roaring-sucking sound of the flames shooting into the sky and the dull cries of the men in the water. Steadfast knew what every man on the ship was thinking: 'Rescue those poor bastards'. He gritted his teeth. At what cost? At the cost of an E-boat escaping? At the cost of *Defiant* being torpedoed while dead in the water? No, the corvette would have to pick them up. His job was to find the E-boat.

Yet in the tense silence of the waiting ship his command 'Full ahead' seemed to ring out and echo as if he had shouted to the heavens: 'Let them drown!'

The engines roared into life and *Defiant* sped off. Not one man spoke.

Steadfast was not going to be fooled into thinking that the boats had departed – there were plenty more torpedoes to come.

'Star shell,' called Steadfast.

The night sky dazzled once more in a firework display fit for a monarch's birthday. A lookout's shout quickly followed:

'E-boat at 30 green.'

The boat lay, apparently stationary, on the edge of the convoy.

'You don't often get such a good look at 100 tons of 40-knot steel,' remarked Steadfast, calmly observing his enemy now at such close quarters.

'Yes, quite a sight,' said Gardiner, 'But it's as deadly as a carnivore on an African plain. Looks like engine trouble, sir.'

'Whatever it is, she's ours!' cried Steadfast over the thundering and crashing of *Defiant*'s 4-inch guns, now spraying the brightly lit sea. A few rounds were enough to find the boat's magazine. A deafening, booming, tearing sound filled the air as flames and debris rose high up into the dark sky and then rained down with a clattering, dripping noise.

'That surprised him!' cried Gardiner.

'Another boat, 70 green!' cried a lookout.

Able seaman Morrison swiftly swung round his Mark VII gun and gave a burst of fire. The rapidly approaching boat seemed to lurch and slow down. A cheer went up from those on *Defiant*'s deck.

Steadfast turned to Gardiner, saying, 'The gunners are on form tonight, Number One. Scruffy they may be, but they know how to punish Jerry.'

'It's as I told you, sir. These men have been through hell in the last twenty-four hours. None of the men at those guns have slept more than the odd hour since we left port, and some are nursing broken ribs and nasty cuts from injuries from the storm. Yet they turn out like the professionals they are.'

With some reluctance, Steadfast muttered, 'Yes, you were right about the men.'

While Steadfast and Gardiner had been discussing the performance of the men, *Defiant* had been gaining on the damaged E-boat, clearly visible from its departing wake of white frothing foam, like the tail of a fleeing rabbit. Morrison turned the forward gun on the fugitive. A volley of shells caught the stern of the escaping boat, blasting off her propellers. The boat stopped dead.

By any rights, Morrison would have kept on firing and sent the boat to the bottom, but just at that moment another boat came racing towards *Defiant*. Swinging round the gun, Morrison opened fire. The first shells fell short, but the boat got the message. Turning on a sixpence it was soon speeding away, zigzagging wildly. Then it disappeared into the darkness beyond the battle area.

When Morrison swung his gun back to the disabled boat and was about to fire again, he saw two men hauling down the ensign. Steadfast, who hadn't missed a shot or a turn of the battle shouted, 'Don't fire!' The boat was surrendering.

'Paris, make up a boarding party.'

'Morrison, cover the boarding party.'

Paris gathered three seaman from the deck. Armed with side-arms and a Lewis gun, they waited in the waist for *Defiant* to approach the damaged E-boat. Its crew showed no sign of being armed and looked rather at a loss as to what to do. What a convoy this was turning out to be, thought Paris. To think that back in Eastborough College later today, some elderly retired teacher would be sitting in front of *my* Lower Sixth Classics set taking the reluctant boys through some Horace or Virgil. Now he, Henry Paris, late of a victorious Cambridge eight on the Thames, was to set foot in a whaleboat to take the surrender of one of the infamous E-boats. It was like a dream. But it was one that, in a moment, could trip into a nightmare.

Although both excited and nervous, it didn't occur to Paris that the rest of the boat party had never taken a surrender either. There was young Norman Wood, who rarely got out of the galley and was scared stiff, but tried not to show it. His stomach churned over, just like it did at home on the big dipper at Blackpool. The rest of the boarding party – Leading Seaman Warren Armstrong, Gunner's mate Joe Callaghan and Ordinary Seaman Eric Sullivan – savoured this moment. Bluffer Armstrong, the ship's poker champion, was always ready to take a risk. Sullivan, who had been down in the sea once from an E-boat attack, was burning to take his revenge. As to Callaghan, he just wanted to see what the bastards really looked like.

'Jerry, here we come!' shouted a triumphant Sullivan.

'Yer, one less bloody E-boat!' called the sardonic Callaghan.

With the boarding party in the whale boat, Paris gave the order to lower the boat, relishing every moment of this conquest. As the boat dipped into the water and pushed off, Wood began to feel the excitement of taking prisoners. What a tale to tell his girlfriend! What a tale to tell the boys down the pub! His fear ebbed away as he became more of fighting seaman.

The E-boat was about two-hundred feet from the *Defiant*. The four men rowed strongly in the unforgiving sea but the whaler approached the stricken E-boat painfully slowly. Paris kept his eyes on the prize – an E-boat that looked undamaged and yet lay marooned before him. Behind him a good part of *Defiant*'s crew had found an excuse to be on deck to watch this moment of triumph. Steadfast hesitated – it wasn't right, all these men not at their posts – another attack could come at any time. Once near to the craft, Paris stood up, one hand still on the tiller, and adopted the sort of commanding stance that he thought fit for the occasion.

Back on the bridge Steadfast was thinking of the other E-boats that were not accounted for; 'Gardiner, telephone the director and guns and make sure they're ready for action.' Then he bent down to the engine room voice pipe and called, 'Chief, all ready for a quick get-away?'

'Aye, aye, sir,' came the reply.

The whaler now lay alongside the E-boat. Paris stood ready to clamber up. As the sea brought the E-boat momentarily lower, he leapt up, grabbed the gunwale and crashed down onto the German deck. Although flat on his back on the deck, the E-boat crew made no attempt to take advantage of his position. Holding his pistol upwards, he stood up, rather bruised and with a searing pain in one ankle. He signalled to the rest of the boarding party to join him.

Armstrong, Wood and Callaghan thumped down on the E-boat deck. Then, before Sullivan, who was holding the Lewis gun, could drop, Paris cried out, 'Stay there and cover us!' He had realised the risk to the Lewis gun if its carrier too smashed down on the E-boat deck.

Now standing erect – or as erect as his ankle would permit – Paris waved his pistol to indicate to the Germans that they were to move towards the stern, ready to be taken off. One by one they slouched aft. So that's what the bastards look like, thought Callaghan: about as cheerful as a bunch of undertakers and as manly as a group of Morris dancers.

'Armstrong, Wood: stand by to assist the prisoners. Callaghan, cover Wood and Armstrong,' ordered an ever more confident Paris.

Paris, having disposed his men to safely cover the transfer of the prisoners to the whaler, positioned himself with a clear line of fire towards the disembarking point. With his pistol in his right hand, he waved forward the first prisoner. Sullenly, the man went over the side and sat glumly in the whaler. One by one his fellows followed.

'Steady does it,' Paris called to Armstrong and Wood as they bunched the prisoners too close for comfort – if he had to shoot, he didn't want to take more than was needed.

Just as Paris was thinking how well the boarding was going, he suddenly realised that there was no sign of the Oberleutnant zur See. He had been at the back of the group when Paris had boarded, but now he was nowhere in sight.

'Armstrong, Wood: go inside and look for the commander. And be careful, he may be armed.'

As the two seamen passed down the boat to the doorway, the German sailors grudgingly stepped aside. Paris turned back to the last few prisoners, taking extra care to keep his distance now that he was alone in the well of the boat.

The loud crack of a gun, shouts and the noise of scuffle from inside the E-boat ended Paris's self-congratulatory musing. Wood came tumbling out onto the deck.

'He's got Armstrong's gun... he's going to...'

Before he could finish his sentence, the air was rent with a thundering, crashing, tearing sound as a gigantic explosion tore the top off the fore part of the E-boat. Paris, thrown to the deck on his back, saw Wood tumbling through the air in the midst of the splintered E-boat.

Chapter 10 – Taking Prisoners

The few remaining prisoners on the E-boat had been thrown into the deep, while the whaler remained unharmed alongside the terminally damaged enemy vessel.

'So, we got the men, but not the boat,' said Gardiner to Steadfast.

'Looks like it, but we're not done yet. Jerry may have some other tricks to surprise us with.'

'Other?'

'Well, you don't think that boat blew up all by itself, do you?'

'Why not?'

'Why bloody not? Didn't you see that Oberleutnant sneak back inside?'

'Can't say that I did, sir.'

'Well he did – and what for? – to sabotage the boat. And I bet it's Wendorff's work.'

'Why, sir?'

'I just sense it. I'm sure he's out there tonight. First the decoy, now the sabotage. We're up against a crack commander tonight.'

Back on the still floating E-boat Callaghan knelt over Paris.

'Are you OK, sir?'

'Sort of, but I think I've broken something.'

'Can you stand?'

'Don't think so. Give me a hand over the side.'

'Sullivan! Need yr' 'elp 'ere!'

'I can't leave this bunch of evil scum! I'll have to go back for help.'

'Wait... we're sinking!'

But Sullivan had no intention of stepping onto the E-boat and leaving nearly twenty prisoners unguarded in the whaler. He pointed to the oars with his Lewis gun. Four reluctant prisoners shuffled onto the thwarts, took up the oars and began the hard tug back to the *Defiant*. A healthy-sized welcome party stood on deck above the scrambling net while the prisoners clambered up resentfully in moody silence.

'Get me two men to bring back Paris,' called Sullivan.

Wilbert Parsons and Sam Hancock slithered down the net, took up a pair of oars and set off for the E-boat. This was young Parsons' first escort run. He had been an unruly lad at school, who never liked to miss a fight or pass up a prank. 'This'll be fun,' he remarked to Hancock. Hancock had seen enough so-called 'fun' in the Great War on the Harwich destroyers, but he liked young Paris and was more than willing to join in his rescue.

In the wild sea they passed some of the Germans thrown off the E-boat by its commander's sabotage.

'We'll get you on the way back,' shouted Sullivan.

'Don't expect the buggers understand you,' remarked Parsons.

'Who cares. It's Paris that matters now,' said Hancock.

'Shut up you two and row. Row, damn you! They're bloody sinking!'

One minute later Sullivan cried out, 'Oh hell, it's gone!'

All that remained of the E-boat was a swirling mass of splintered wood – and two heads bobbing in the water.

'Row, row …!'

As the whaler neared the two men, Sullivan was already crouched over the prow, leaning out to grab Callaghan.

'Take Paris – he's hurt,' cried Callaghan.

Sullivan and Parsons grabbed the sub lieutenant under the shoulders and heaved his dripping body on board. As Paris lay on the bottom of the boat, he whispered, 'We did it!' and lapsed into unconsciousness.

Callaghan, by now excited at his adventure and billowing with pride at having succoured the sub lieutenant, scrambled on board unaided.

Hancock and Parsons, back on the oars, rowed slowly through the mass of debris, while Sullivan steered from one to another of the three Germans still alive in the water. Of Wood, there was no sign. Parsons took a keen interest in his charges, while Callaghan scowled at having to share a boat with a hated enemy.

Back at the ship the Germans reluctantly struggled up the nets, while Paris was hauled up on a rope. No sooner had the whaler been attached to the falls than Steadfast called, 'Full ahead, Chief.'

***

Once more on the edge of the convoy, *Defiant* settled down to see the night hours out in the lull after the attack. Down below on the unheated mess decks men who had been on deck were stripping off wet clothing and putting on drier and, most importantly, warmer clothing. This was no time for fashion or decorum. Anything that they could lay their hands on – overcoats, oilskins, working overalls – was put to use.

But the real enemy was tiredness. After the adrenalin rush of battle, the accumulated tiredness of years of war, of watch-keeping and hard living, caught up with them. In quiet times like these they were overcome with the boredom and monotony of the routine of patrols and convoys. Tonight, exhausted as the men were, few could sleep. Too tired to go on, but too tired to switch off, they dozed in corners, on benches and on top of stores. It was beyond what human flesh was meant to endure.

Under attack or in the danger zones of E-boat alley, the unremitting exposure to peril frayed men's nerves. Sparks had still not been told about his predecessor, who had crumpled under the pressure and was carried off the ship yelling out orders to the officers on the bridge and declaring himself to be a rear admiral. And then there was the strain on the body. Leave was so brief and so rare that one harassing convoy followed another in an unremitting grind.

The officers, too, now fell into a state of post-battle inertia. The urgency of action, the tension of keeping watch, the terror behind the faint sound of a motor or an unidentified streak across the sea, took men to the limits of their powers. They were living on reserves of nervous energy, reserves that could only be dipped into in the heat of action. But each dipping diminished those reserves.

Steadfast alone felt invigorated by the night. Even so, he was seeing double after thirty-six hours without any solid sleep. Yet he was also dreaming of the recognition he would receive for capturing an E-boat crew. How many times had it been done before, he wondered. Once perhaps?

And the weather was never the convoy's friend. Clear skies exposed them to attack from a brutal foe; from the air, on surface and from below. Fog and mist could mean collision, or simply the fear-ridden boredom of anxiously lying at anchor, fearing attack at any moment. As to the night hours, nothing could be lonelier and more wearying; hour after hour in total darkness on deck and not one friendly light shining from the shore.

In fact the crew were like zombies, worn down physically and mentally. Digestive conditions were rife from indifferent food and hurried eating. Many men were losing teeth and had infected gums.

There was not one man on the ship who could be said to be truly operationally effective.

Steadfast knew all this as well as his men. Around three in the morning he had seen the strain on Ross, who had ordered the helmsman to turn fifteen degrees to starboard to tighten up the convoy. The wheel went over and stayed over. When Steadfast stepped onto the bridge the ship was making a good attempt at a circle and Ross was asleep on his feet.

'Are you going to complete the circle, Sub Lieutenant?'

Ross jumped and gave orders to straighten up.

Ross wasn't the only man who was fighting exhaustion. Steadfast could hear the director and guns calling to each other every so often, just to keep each other awake.

And tomorrow, we've got to sort out the mess of this convoy, thought Steadfast.

'Ross, go and get some sleep. I'm going to need you at daylight.'

Chapter 11- Order out of Chaos

A cold grey dawn gradually gave way to the first flecks of amber sunlight as Steadfast stepped onto the bridge after attempting but failing to sleep. He slumped onto his high chair and watched as colour slowly returned to the ship. First, glints of silver picked out the aerials, still miraculously in place after the storm. Then the yellow of the men's oilskins began to glow softly. Next the daylight caught the red of the lifebuoys. The sea too began now to show its greys and greens, with touches of white foam and yellow glints from the low rays of the sun. Another long hard night was over and the ship was returning to her normal daily routine. He relished this time of day at sea in war as he prepared for the excitements and hazards to come – even a day without his midshipman, Kendrick having declared Beverton unfit for the rest of the voyage.

Steadfast stirred his exhausted frame and slid off his chair into a standing position. He attempted a few feeble stretches but his body refused to respond. He settled for leaning on the rail in a barely conscious state. His numb hands fumbled for his glasses. Listlessly he raised them to his eyes and surveyed the misty sea in the cold early light. Where there had been two neat columns of merchant ships he now saw an incoherent array of wanderers. The E-boat attack had left the convoy in chaos. Some colliers had put on speed, some had held back, some had kept the course, others had veered off into the darkness. Some, he assumed, had sunk, but he knew nothing of them. In the far distance he could make out two colliers listing drunkenly and a third seemed to be stationary. He would leave the *Keswick* to sort them out.

Ahead was an empty sea. So Rawlinson *had* rushed off in the night and probably knew nothing of the attack. He must have taken the first ten or so ships. By now he was doubtless doing 10-knots. Steadfast had no other choice than to declare himself commodore of the rear convoy.

But what a convoy! It was spread out over perhaps fifteen miles of length and he had no idea what width it was. The two orderly columns of cargo ships, tucked comfortably into the marked channel, were now as widely dispersed as the currants in a penny bun.

His first job was to pull the convoy together.

***

Gardiner reappeared on the bridge just as the hot coffee that Steadfast had ordered arrived.

'Good morning, Number One.'

Gardiner returned the greeting and asked, 'How's the convoy looking?'

'Between the commodore and Jerry we've been left in an almighty mess. The commodore's not to be seen. Heaven knows how far ahead he is, but we're on our own now. We won't race him,' replied Steadfast.

'Can we manage, sir?'

'That's not a question which we have the luxury to ask ourselves, Number One. Somehow we've got to get whatever's left of the convoy to Tilbury, commodore or no commodore.'

'Just us?'

'*Defiant* and the corvette. It looks as if the commodore's taken *Tremendous* with him.'

'And what do we do for a commodore?'

'That's me now. I've no choice but to take over.'

Steadfast was more than a little pleased at this thought. He'd come out of the last night rather well with two E-boats disposed of (even if one was with a little bit of help from Jerry) and *Defiant* was still in fighting form. The men had turned out rather well. It was a pity about Paris. He'd done splendidly. He had even sent two men after the E-boat commander. It was not his fault that the commander was just that bit ahead in his thinking. And perhaps the absence of *Tremendous* was of little consequence. She didn't seem to be around when needed last night. On balance, better to go on alone and so leave the Admiralty in no doubt as to who had won through. Thank God Ross was in one piece – he would keep his old Whitehall friends informed of *Defiant*'s triumphs.

Steadfast straightened himself up and looked out to sea, surveying what he could locate of the merchantmen. He might have lost a few ratings and have a midshipman out of commission, but he wasn't going to lose a convoy.

'Time to get to work, Number One. Those men out there have put their faith in us. We're not going to let them down.'

61

'If you say so, sir,' replied Gardiner, his mind still on the weakness of the escort after the night's depredations.

'Come on now, Number One, buck up! We've a big job on our hands this morning pulling this lot into some sort of order.' As he said this, Steadfast waved his right arm in a derisory manner in a vaguely northward direction, where he presumed the convoy lay scattered.'

'We'll slow down the convoy to 5-knots.'

'Five?' gasped Gardiner.

'Yes, five. It's our only hope of pulling the blasted convoy together. Then, we chase down to the rear, getting the ships to close up. When we've found the last straggler, we'll come back up at 10-knots – that gives us a better chance to deal with those bloody-minded masters who don't like taking orders. There's always some idiot who thinks he can make it by himself.'

'And then?'

'Well, we should be back at the head of the convoy by midday and then, with luck, we can resume our 7-knots.'

'And if Jerry attacks while we're rounding up the sheep?'

'Gardiner, I really don't know. All I know is that we can't just steam on when the convoy's about as big as the Isle of Wight.'

***

Steadfast chose two ships to head the two new columns and gave them their course with firm instructions not to exceed 5-knots until the *Defiant* returned to take over the commodore's position.

'What are those two masters fussing about, Number One?'

'5-knots, sir.'

'Why?'

Gardiner, rather pleased to see how much more he knew about convoys than Steadfast did, explained: 'Lots of colliers won't answer the rudder at that speed. Their masters are worried they won't be able to keep their ships heading on the course.'

Steadfast shrugged his shoulders and growled, 'Umf. Fussy old lot. Never happy. Oh well, they'll have to manage as best they can. We're off on a straggler hunt. Tally-ho!'

Gardiner inwardly winced at Steadfast's hunting reference. It all seemed rather flippant, even un-naval, to him.

Defiant proceeded back down the convoy, searching out those ships that could be found and giving them each a new position. It was slow work since Steadfast had to be sure that each master understood his orders before he moved on to the next. With no commodore and the convoy long having lost the sequence set to facilitate early departures, the best he could do was to bunch the ships back into a manageable formation. The niceties of a neatly ordered convoy were now unthinkable.

He reckoned the convoy was several miles wide by now so he zigzagged across it in search of all the outliers, ordering them back in. It was some hours before he found the *Keswick* at the end of the convoy – fifteen miles from where he had started and perhaps twenty from where the commodore now was. He marvelled at just how far the convoy had spread in so few hours.

***

'Let's hope we're all back together now. Eighteen ships,' said Steadfast as *Defiant* turned south to take up the leader's position.

'I wonder how many the commodore has,' mused Gardiner.

'I reckon we've lost at least three, so he can't have more than fourteen. He won't have noticed, though. He ploughs on without asking what's going on behind. Lucky for him we're here to sort out his messes.'

As the *Defiant* came back up the convoy, Gardiner called out, 'Something's wrong, sir. Look at that gap!'

Over on the coastal side of the convoy there was a huge breach in the column – enough for several ships.

'Can't have been sunk. They must have gone AWOL.'

'Damn! It's that buoy ten miles back, where the channel turns. They've missed it. They'll soon realise, won't they, sir?'

'Yes – but not in the way you mean. They're heading straight for the Eastforth sandbank.'

Steadfast went to the engine room voice pipe: 'Full ahead.'

'Steer two-two-five.'

'Are we going after them?'

'Yes, but I reckon we're too late. They've at most twenty minutes before they hit the sandbank.'

Defiant raced through the convoy, her powerful wake rocking each collier as she passed and leaving behind puzzled masters as they watched their protector sprint away from them.

'Ships on the port bow, sir,' called a lookout.

'We're too late, sir. Look!'

There on the Eastforth sandbank were three beached colliers with wisps of black smoke coming from their now useless engines. Steadfast could see men on the decks, peering over the side at the shallow water below.

'Not too close, helmsman. Keep clear of the sandbank.'

'Ahoy there,' shouted Steadfast through a megaphone.

A couple of masters appeared, one with a megaphone, who replied, 'We're stuck.'

'Rather too obvious,' responded Steadfast in a voice that conveyed his contempt for this display of incompetent seamanship.

'What shall we do?' asked Gardiner.

'Nothing. We can't hang around here. Their men will have to row themselves ashore – it's near enough – or they could wait for the Lifeboat Service.'

'Odd, isn't it,' said Gardiner, 'how the lifeboats have become more or less a taxi service out here in the war?'

'Rather predictable from what I've seen of these East Coast merchantmen,' replied Steadfast.

'Yeoman, make a signal to the merchantmen. Will report your position. Suggest you wait for lifeboat.'

'Quartermaster, steer one-three-five until we reach the middle of the convoy. Then resume course to the head of the convoy.'

'Bit of a rough one, this convoy, isn't it, sir?' remarked Gardiner.

'You could say that,' replied Steadfast, inwardly thinking that a rough convoy was a good convoy. But his taste for adventure was soon to be tested again.

Chapter 12 – A Visit from the Luftwaffe

By early afternoon the convoy was once more proceeding southwards in a rough but tolerable order. Despite its ragged appearance there was an air of contentment about the small ships sitting low in a choppy sea. White slipstreams of foam at their bows contrasted with the dark grey water. The wind was breaking the surface into swelling waves, some dark, others dazzlingly yellow as they caught the low rays of the winter sun. The ships moved silently as one, as if magically propelled by some mighty invisible hand. Only the smoke streaming behind the mostly coal-burning vessels betrayed the urgent purpose of the convoy.

'Not so rough this afternoon, sir,' observed Ross.

'No. The sea won't be our enemy now. It's the sky's turn. The Luftwaffe will be on the prowl. We'll need to double the lookouts. With luck we'll have a chance to show them what the Navy's made of.'

The sound of clumping footsteps on the ladder caused Steadfast to turn. He was astonished to see Paris awkwardly heaving himself up onto the bridge.

'Reporting for duty, sir.'

'But I thought…'

'The doc says there's nothing broken – something about ligaments. He's sort of trussed up my leg, but I can move about.'

'I never turn away a volunteer. You think you're up to standing watches?'

'Sir!'

'OK, but if you need to "sit" your watch, you've my permission to do so.'

'Thank you, sir.'

'You can take over from Ross later.'

Paris struggled back down the ladder, his progress impeded by his right leg being as stiff as a cannon's ramrod.

'Well, well,' said Steadfast, 'I think I've misjudged that lad.'

'I think we all have,' agreed Gardiner, 'in a month or two no one will believe he's only a dressed up schoolmaster.'

***

The calmer sea gave Steadfast a chance to assess the damage from the collision and the storm. Aft the guardrails had been carried away as if torn off by the massive teeth of a resurrected dinosaur. Miscellaneous stanchions had been reduced to ragged stumps and large sections of splinter plating had been mangled into contorted shapes by the force of the mighty sea. A good deal of the lashed-down gear – smoke floats, cables, axes – had been brutally ripped from their mountings. Nothing too vital there, Steadfast reassured himself. Best not to think about the missing boat even if the loss of some of the abandon-ship gear was a little more serious. As to the disappearance of Ordinary Seaman Langton and the loss of Armstrong and Wood in the E-boat explosion, that was just part of the price of war. Yes, *Defiant* remained a fighting machine in full working order and *he* was in command.

***

Around 2.00 pm Steadfast first heard the faintest of drones in the east. The sun was streaking through the broken cloud as he raised his glasses to search the sky. Then he saw it. He sharpened the focus and carefully studied the plane's vague outline against a patch of blue sky. He knew it well. It was a Dornier Do 17, clearly recognisable with its shoulder wing structure and twin tail. There's a worthy foe, thought Steadfast: speedy, manoeuvrable and a fearful opponent at low altitude. Many a ship had been taken by surprise by a Do 17 seemingly appearing from nowhere. Momentarily he wondered whether *Defiant*'s gunners were good enough to hit that slender airframe. Then he asked himself how he could doubt them after last night's showing.

While mentally preparing himself for an air attack, Steadfast noticed that the plane was keeping its altitude. Reconnaissance, he realised. Last night's visitors had passed on the message. The convoy had been spotted again. Already its size, course and position would have been radioed back to a Luftwaffe base and German aircrew would be running to their planes.

It was not until mid afternoon that a lookout heard the first distant sound of several aeroplane engines. 'Aircraft approaching abaft port!' yelled the excited port bridge lookout. He was astounded when Steadfast responded with a calm and quiet, 'Well, sound the air attack alarm,' as calmly as he might ask for a mug of cocoa. Ever since the reconnaissance plane had passed over, he had known his visitors would come. And he knew what it might mean for him as the nagging pain from a piece of Narvik shrapnel in his left shoulder reminded him. He had a score to settle and welcomed the moment to fight back from the depths of his being.

As the ship went to action stations, Steadfast raised his glasses and scanned the eastward sky, his eyes dazzled by the bright sunshine breaking through the patches in the cloud. The plane was about ten miles away. He watched as it rapidly grew nearer. Then he realised it was not alone. How many planes? Two? He looked again.

'Ross, take a look. Two planes, do you reckon?'

Ross had been following the sighting too. He looked more closely. Left eye. Right eye. Both eyes.

'Three, sir. Look quite high to me.'

Yes, thought Steadfast. They're not keen to come too close to our guns. It's good to know they're not suicidal types.

And then they came – three Heinkels He 111.

'Commence zigzagging, Quartermaster,' ordered Steadfast.

He had ordered Cole to the wheel as soon as he knew that action was imminent. Only a quartermaster was well-enough trained to throw the ship about to dodge bombs without capsizing her.

Steadfast knew that *Defiant* was ready. She was a marvel of the latest technology and nothing was more up-to-date about her than her gun control. The sizeable target of a plane was just what the director was for. The guns would follow with an accuracy no man could match.

The planes were fast approaching as the men in the gun emplacements fed the first shells into the fuse setters to pick up the fuse length from the director. Then slam went the first 35-pound shell into the breech loader.

'Guns, get the range,' called out Steadfast. 'All guns follow director. Don't fire until I order.'

Guns kept the director trained on the planes as they came towards *Defiant*. 'Range 12,000, sir.'

'Range 10,000.'

'Fire!' yelled Steadfast.

In the forward gun emplacement half a dozen men worked at each of the two guns, their every move carried out in a smooth synchronised rhythm – the reward for hour after hour of practice. Deftly and speedily they fed their machine of death. Up came a shell. Into the fuse-setting tray to pick up the range from the director. Slam into breech. Crash went the breech block. Fire. Grab the next shell…

There was a deafening roar, and flashes of blinding orange from the guns. With each firing the ship appeared to stagger backwards under the blast. Men's ears seemed ready to explode and their lungs felt as if they were bursting as they choked back the smell of cordite. Down below, the ship shook as if it were being tossed in a giant colander. Each ear-splitting round after ear-splitting round seemed to penetrate to the very marrow of the men's bones. The bitter smell of cordite began to filter down to the bowels of the ship. The sea sprouted fountains of water as the shrapnel fell from the sky. Meanwhile the pom-poms were banging away like pneumatic drills. The whole ship seemed to spout fire, smoke and explosions like a 4th July firework display.

Steadfast watched as the sticks of bombs spewed from the Heinkel bomb bays, falling, turning over, looking so harmless up in the sky. There was the first, over by the small tramp with the low funnel. He tensed himself for the hit. But no, the slow un-manoeuvrable steamer slid before the bomb, which fell harmlessly 20-yards behind it, throwing up a pillar of water high above the convoy. And then another, this time much nearer to the port side of the convoy. It fell with a screaming whistle before it too dropped into the sea. Steadfast welcomed the wind-born spray as it wet his face. It was like a baptism of his new role as commander in battle, a proof of his manly inheritance of the Navy's tradition of commanders standing boldly on the quarterdeck under fire. Supressing the tiredness that wracked his body, he straightened up as he imagined himself standing by Nelson's side at Trafalgar.

Suddenly Steadfast realised that the *Defiant* was the next target. He could see the bomb coming down right ahead of the ship. It was tumbling in a way that seemed almost leisurely. But he was not deceived.

'Hard to port,' he calmly called, all the while standing easy.

The ship lurched to his command.

'Full ahead.'

The bomb fell two yards to starboard, throwing up a fountain of water that fell back like a tidal wave on the *Defiant*, drenching the men on the station aft. On the bridge the officers and men shook off their soaking coats, wiped their glasses and anxiously turned their gaze back to the sky. Another bomb! This time to port. This Jerry knew his business. A bomb had got the better of Steadfast once; now he was determined to get even.

'Hard to starboard!'

Defiant was now moving at speed. The ship obeyed his orders like one of Steadfast's field hunter's that responded to every flick of his riding whip and every touch of his spurs. As she turned she heeled over and cut into the writhing sea. Ten seconds of terror spread through the ship. Down below, the engine room men had felt the first jolt when the *Defiant* was barely moving. This time a stoker was thrown across the engine room and another's hand was torn from the valve he was adjusting. He grabbed a stanchion and held his breath. There was a tinkling of glass as various lanterns shattered under the violent shocks and some of the lights went out. *Defiant* creaked under the strain of her brutal manoeuvre. No one said a word, other than a muttered prayer. One second, two seconds, three.... ten. The bomb must have missed.

Missed, but only just. One torpedo man claimed to have heard the bomb scrape the side of the ship. But the damage was no more than another cascade of freezing water. As the last frothing rivulets fell back into the sea, Steadfast glanced up. The planes were gone.

'Course one-two-five. One-hundred revolutions,' he calmly called as he brought the ship back to normality.

''e's a cool one,' remarked Elphick.

'Yer, 'e never ducked once. Just kept looking at the bombs as they came down. Reckon 'e's as tough as he looks,' replied Greenwood.

'Let's 'ope 'e's not too tough,' quipped Elphick.

***

The three bombers departed, leaving the convoy shocked and disrupted. Steadfast ordered, 'Resume course,' and the cargo ships began to straighten up again. It had been a rather feeble high altitude attack, with little chance of hitting the relatively small vessels in the vast sea. Steadfast wondered whether that was all that the spotter plane had called up. Or had the bombers stumbled on the convoy by chance?

'We saw them off, didn't we, sir?' remarked Ross.

'We did. But I don't think that's it for today.'

'Why not?'

'Think about it. A spotter plane reports our position and all Jerry sends us is three high-level bombers with not much hope of a hit. And here we are cruising along at a pathetic 7-knots under a clear sky, sticking out like a billboard in Piccadilly Circus. Doesn't make sense.'

'So you reckon there'll be more?'

'For certain. That lot must have been up when the call came. We were just an extra job on their run home. Mark my words, the real thing will soon be here. We'll stay closed up at action stations.'

Confirmation of Steadfast's forecast came half an hour later when the port lookout once more called out, 'Aircraft on the port bow!'

Steadfast looked up and saw the planes, low in the sky and descending steadily.

'Torpedo bombers,' he remarked calmly to Ross.

Ross had only been in one torpedo bomber attack. It was just three weeks into his time on *Defiant*. It had been the most terrifying moment of his life. He had no idea what was the worst thing about these attacks: the speed of the approaching enemy, the sight of the racing torpedo, the petrifying feeling as the departing planes screamed over the ship? The one thing that was certain was that such an attack left men traumatised.

Steadfast watched as the next wave of Heinkels came in at around 250 miles per hour. Lower and lower they came, rushing towards the east side of the convoy. He knew this horrific moment too well. From a plane's first blip on the horizon it was only minutes to seeing its lethal load ominously slung beneath it. Then, seconds later, the plane was skimming the masthead. You counted those chilling seconds, wondering whether you had escaped the torpedo. If not... Ugh! Yes, he knew all about 'if not'. A cold shiver ran through him as the sounds and sights that visited him in the depths of the night welled-up in his imagination. Steadfast shook himself back to the present.

The first plane came in well to the north of *Defiant* and then turned towards the convoy.

'We're not the target,' remarked Gardiner, who was now on the bridge.

'Not this time,' replied Steadfast.

'Poor sods – that collier's in for it!'

'Looks like it. She can't dodge the torpedoes as well as we can. But lots of them have got good guns now: 12-pounder quick-firers plus an Oerlikon. They've all got Navy gunners – there, look at that.'

They were watching a largish collier, right in the path of the first torpedo plane. The machine was no more than two hundred feet above the sea, screaming down on the merchantman. But ahead of it was a wall of tracer, AA shells and machine gun fire. It seemed impossible that the plane could survive. Then a burst of flame came from its fuselage. The plane wobbled a bit but the pilot quickly regained control. The AA fire from the collier and *Defiant* continued to burst around the tiny plane. For a few more seconds it kept its path. Then, 'splat!' as a large chunk of the tail blasted off. The plane swerved erratically and the panicking pilot released his torpedo. But he had turned too quickly and the torpedo ran harmlessly ahead of the collier. *Defiant* and the collier gave one more burst of needless fire. Already, the plane was spiralling down out of control into the sea.

'OK so far,' remarked Steadfast.

The second plane peeled off, dropping in height more quickly. Steadfast watched, knowing exactly the pilot's intent: his target was *Defiant*, out on the port side. Lower and lower it came towards its target of the 300 feet of *Defiant*'s beam – a near unmissable target. It was only a couple of minutes away.

Johnson on the port Oerlikon watched as the plane came hurtling towards him. At masthead height its thin profile presented a hopelessly small target. His gun was not controlled by the director so he had to aim by sight. On and on it came. Johnson felt his hands tremble in terror and he feared he would lose control of his gun. Seen in his sights the attack by the approaching plane felt personal, as if *he* alone were the target. In a rush of righteous anger Johnson cried out, 'No you don't!' and let out a burst of fire. 'Die, you bugger, die!'

Suddenly he heard Steadfast call, 'Hard to port. Stop port engine.' A swell of relief passed through Johnson as he realised that Steadfast was bringing the ship round.

Steadfast had almost no time at all to bring *Defiant*'s prow round to face the aircraft, reducing the target she offered to the mere 33 feet of her beam. Thrashing in the water, *Defiant* heeled over, over,…. Now careering almost directly towards the plane, her AA swinging round to keep its lethal fire on the aircraft. The pilot saw that he had been outmanoeuvred. Up went his stick and the plane pulled away, in a storm of tracer and pom-pom bullets.

'Return to course. Continue zigzagging,' Steadfast calmly called.

But the plane was not done. It flew on over and beyond the convoy. Still rising, it circled and began to return back across the colliers, this time to attack *Defiant*'s starboard side. The plane began to descend. Soon it reached the western edge of the convoy by which time it was barely clearing the mast tops. The guns on the merchantmen were pounding away and black puffs of smoke burst around the Heinkel. Undeterred, the pilot held *Defiant* in his sights and hurled his plane towards her.

Now the plane was just a few hundred feet from the ship. *Defiant* was swinging round as Steadfast brought her stern-on to the plane, leaving behind a huge circle of white foaming wake. The director kept the guns locked on the approaching plane as the ship twisted around. The men on the deck were deafened by the thunder of the 4-inch guns and the drumming bangs of the pom-pom. Yet still the plane kept coming.

Defiant's crew prepared for the hit. The plane was so low, so close, so straight, nothing could save them. A torpedo strike full on the stern would surely tear the ship apart in minutes.

When the plane was no more than one-hundred feet from *Defiant*, with its menacing torpedo still hanging underneath the fuselage, Ross suddenly shouted: 'It's jammed – the torpedo's jammed!' jumping up and down in excitement. (Steadfast noted with derision this un-Naval performance – not what he expected from an *Admiralty* man.)

Before anyone could reply, the nose of the plane jerked up as if the pilot was trying to gain altitude. There was a burst of orange fire and smoke from the engine and the plane began to twist. Then it turned to plunge nose-downwards as the pilot lost control. He managed a final lift just before he reached the ship but at that moment *Defiant*'s AA ripped off one wing, which spun off like an empty cigarette packet flung from a car window. The out of control plane was now plunging towards *Defiant*, twisting like a demented corkscrew. (The torpedo had fallen harmlessly into the sea beside the ship.)

But *Defiant* was not out of danger. Men ran for cover as the plane crashed nose-first onto the deck and burst into flames.

The fuselage and wings had been torn apart by the impact. Pieces of bodywork, bolts, bits of instruments, pipes and valves tore across the flats and ripped into *Defiant*'s pipes, wires and fittings. The two men at the starboard depth-charges fell to the deck as their flesh was lacerated by flying metal. Several men were blasted off the deck into the sea. The fresh-faced Gunner Owens, who had been cheering the demise of the plane, disappeared in a ball of flame, without ever seeing the daughter born to him the day before. His mate, Joe Callaghan, went the same way, so relieving him of the seasickness that had wracked him all night long. Three other seaman at the gun stumbled across the deck. The handsome face of lady's man Fred Carter was burnt beyond recognition; Noah Oldridge fell to the deck with one arm almost torn from his body; and young Toby Higgins, apparently unharmed, fell dead from shock in the arms of Leading Seaman Warren Armstrong.

Chapter 13 – Fire Aft

'Fire party aft,' ordered Steadfast. 'Lookouts keep on maximum alert. There may be more to come.'

The rear of the ship was quickly engulfed in flames and black smoke but Steadfast could already see Paris directing the fire party of Sullivan, Davies, Birch and Slingsby. Never before had these men, who had practised the fire routine so many times, faced a real fire – a fire that threatened their own lives. Without a word Sullivan and Birch each connected a coupling to a hydrant, while the silent Davies and Slingsby grabbed a nozzle and ran out the hoses. After opening the valves, Sullivan and Birch ran back to help play the powerful jets of water onto the flames. As Paris directed the four men, they appeared and disappeared in clouds of choking black smoke.

Paris was already beginning to feel the effects of the flaming wreck. His eyes stung, his lungs were filling with the hot burning gases, and every breath brought searing pains in his chest. A few months ago he had been testing boys on Caesar's Gallic Wars. Now he was being tested by Hitler's Teutonic war. Standing on the flaming deck, his thin fair hair blown into a tangle, the hesitant youth suddenly felt a new strength – the strength of a man – rise within him. He realised that the ship, the men, the captain, all now depended on him. He straightened up as best he could with his ramrod leg, metaphorically filling out his spluttering chest as he felt a fresh sense of command swelling up within him.

It was at that moment that Paris saw the three men trapped aft by the fire. There was Elphick, a bit of a wide boy, but always ready with a tip for the 2.30 when in harbour; Greenwood, his colleague, never to be caught without a smutty story to share; and Ordinary Seaman Sam Peacock, a shirker if ever there was – Paris had caught him only yesterday smoking behind a gun when he should have been cleaning out the heads, and had put him up for Captain's defaulters. Paris stretched out an arm as if trying to reach the men, but no one could cross the flaming barricade that ran across the deck. Before the men or Paris could think what to do, a sudden change in the wind sent a blast of hot, flaming gases aft. In a moment, bits of the three men's clothing were set alight, their hair singed while they all felt the searing heat on their flesh. The three men turned and plunged into the churning wake of the ship.

Gardiner had watched the progress of the fire from the bridge, while Steadfast conned the ship.

'Three men overboard, sir!'

'Stop engines,' ordered Steadfast.

'Boat party, sir?' asked Gardiner.

'Not if we can help it. We're already a sitting target. We can't afford to hang around. Lines only.'

Steadfast worried. Was he right to stop? Was he softening? He excused his weakness on the grounds that it would only take a minute or so to pick up the men now that the sea was calmer. But he knew the risk.

'Chief, stand by to move off in an instant. We've men overboard.'

Paris left the fire fighting party and limped to the edge of the ship. He could see two men waving and a third looking more dead than alive. Leading Seaman Elton threw out three lifebuoys secured to lines.

Peacock, yesterday's shirker, didn't shirk on his own behalf but swam strongly towards one of the lifebuoys and quickly wriggled into it. Without waiting for the men on board to haul him in, he struck out vigorously towards the ship and was quickly pulled up on deck. Elphick, too, had no difficulty in reaching a lifebuoy and slipping into it, but, as he turned towards the ship, he could see the men on board pointing away to the sea. They were shouting something, but he could hear nothing. He turned to where they were pointing and saw Greenwood, who was making no effort to reach the lifebuoy. Fighting the choppy waves, Elphick battled his way over to Greenwood and grabbed him under one arm. The men on the ship had watched and understood. As soon as Elphick had a grip on Greenwood, they began to pull gently on the line to bring the two men to the side of the ship. They hauled up the deadweight of Greenwood onto the deck, where he lay motionless in a pool of oily water. Elphick scrambled up a net and sank down in exhaustion on the deck.

Steadfast had watched every moment of the rescue. He had no intention of waiting one second longer than was needed. As soon as the two men came up out of the sea, he called, 'Half ahead'. *Defiant* lurched into life as the Chief used all his skill to speed her on her way.

Paris had already sent orders for Gibbs to be called up from below and he handed the three cold, shocked and soaking men into his charge.

While the men were being rescued from the sea, the fire party had continued to battle with the flaming plane. It must have been low on fuel since the fire was soon under control and most of the damage was to the plane. Half an hour later the last bits of charred machine were heaved over the side.

'What's the damage, Number One?' asked Steadfast.

'Four dead. Half a dozen badly injured. And the rear gun's looking like the remnants of bonfire night. Shall we pull out, sir?'

'Pull out? We've a convoy to protect. As long as we've guns to fire and men to fire them, we're staying.'

'But have we enough fire-power?'

'What's enough? You fight with what you've got. As long as I'm on the bridge, we stand by the convoy and we fight to the last gun and the last man if we have to. There's only two ways out as far as I'm concerned: either we sink or we're ordered home. Otherwise we stay.'

'And the wounded, sir?'

'The PMO will have to do what he can. I can see you don't look happy, Gardiner, but look at it like this. Suppose we pull out and half an hour later Jerry comes and sinks a merchant man. What would you say to her captain if you met him in a pub a few days later?'

'I see your point, sir. I suppose we fight to the last round?'

'Not just the last round. We fight to the last man and the last moment the ship's afloat. This is war, Number One. Remember what old Jacky Fisher said about war?'

'Can't say that I do.'

'In war, be "Ruthless, Relentless, Remorseless". It's the only way to win.'

'Yes, sir,' replied a reluctant Gardiner.

'And, by the way, Number One, never let the men see your indecision or hesitation. They won't fight if they think *we've* not got the guts to see it through.'

Chapter 14 – Time for Congratulations

That evening a semblance of dinner was offered in the wardroom. Steadfast had seen enough of the intensity of East Coast convoy work to allow him to relax his standards a little. Peters looked rather grubby and there was no clean tablecloth. As to his officers, they looked (and were) exhausted.

'A couple of months back I thought I'd seen the worst when we lost two colliers. But this trip beats the lot,' remarked Gardiner.

'Well, it's war, isn't it?' retorted Steadfast.

'No one needs reminding of that, sir, least of all those poor merchantmen,' Gardiner continued, 'but some runs are worse than others. And this is the worst of the lot.'

Paris burst in on the exchange: 'At least we've taken a plane and seen the end of two E-boats.'

'So we have Paris, and no one will forget your part…'

'Oh, I wasn't suggesting anything like that, sir. I just think we shouldn't fuss about a rather hot run. Anyway, I feel much more confident about *Defiant* now.'

'We all do, I think,' said Ross, 'the ship and the men have put up a great show. Jerry's had a few nasty rebuffs in the last two days.'

'Yes, gentlemen, I think we're all agreed: *Defiant* is a ship to be reckoned with,' responded Steadfast.

'Perhaps she should have been called *Invincible*,' suggested Sherman.

'Go easy! That's not always proved to be a lucky name,' said Steadfast.

'How come?' asked Sherman.

'Well one *Invincible* was wrecked, if I remember rightly. And, of course, the last one was sunk at the Battle of Jutland. Best to stick to *Defiant*, I think. We're the first of that name, so there are no nasty skeletons in our cupboard.'

'A toast to *Defiant*!' called Ross.

***

But *Defiant* had other troubles than the enemy. Down in the mess Elton and Able Seaman Oakshaw had been bickering and sparing all evening. Suddenly their quarrel took a serious turn. They had been arguing over their contribution to the rescue of the three men overboard, when Oakshaw suddenly burst out:

'You're a fucking bastard, Elton. I know all about you and my sister.'

'What about your sister?'

'Well, you're going out with her, ain't you?'

'So what?'

'So bloody what? I'll tell you so bloody what. I know what happened to that Mary Sheldrake girl.'

'What?'

'Just that you bloody got her in the family way.'

'Say that again, you bastard! Just say that again!'

'Like I said, you got her in the family way. And it will be our Mary next.'

'You...'

Elton seized a knife and lunged at Oakshaw across the table. Had Elton been alone on his side of the table, or the table narrower, Oakshaw would have had four-inches of steel in his chest in a moment. But two seamen grabbed the attacker, tore the knife from him, and yanked his arms round his back. In one swift movement they pulled him to the deck and sat on him.

'Get Phillips,' shouted one of the two men.

A short while later Phillips knocked on the wardroom door.

'Sir, bit of trouble below,' he reported to Steadfast.

'What sort of trouble?'

'It's Elton, sir. Seems he's being going out with Oakshaw's sister. Oakshaw said something to upset Elton, and Elton set on him with a knife.'

'Is Oakshaw hurt?'

'No, sir. Two men grabbed Elton. They've got him now.'

'Lock him up him. I'll deal with him tomorrow.'

Steadfast turned from this irritating incident – sailors were always quarrelling – to the troubles of the convoy and his search for the enemy. By morning he had forgotten about Elton – a lapse that was to have serious consequences.

Later, on the bridge, Steadfast and Ross continued the self-congratulatory mood of the dinner conversation.

'Only one more night,' said Ross.

'Yes, tomorrow we should have this rabble safely in the Thames. Then they can fend for themselves,' replied Steadfast.

'We've put up a good show.'

'Not bad,' responded Steadfast. On the downside he was returning minus who knows how many ships and with a seriously damaged stern. Also, Beverton had somehow ended up in the water. But he reckoned the admiral would overlook all this when he heard about the two E-boats. And, by the time Rawlinson had explained how he had lost most of his convoy, Steadfast's return in the joint role of Commodore and Senior Officer Escort should prove a triumph.

Feeling more than pleased about his command Steadfast looked out into the darkness over the swelling sea. He could just make out the lighter patches where a mist hung a few feet above the water, but the patches were well spaced out. If the mist thickened, they would have to drop a knot or two. The thought of slowing down the convoy sent a shiver down his spine.

'120 revolutions, Chief.'

'Course one-seven-oh, Helmsman.'

'We should be passing the northbound convoy any time now,' said Ross.

Steadfast was dreading this moment. He would be powerless to control or direct the merchantmen as they passed in the night. Two convoys of forty or more ships in total, only yards apart in the darkness and without lights, trapped between sandbanks on one side and a minefield on the other. Many masters were not up to this kind of work. They had spent their lives plodding up and down a near empty sea, never having to think about collisions or navigation. Now, stuck in the convoys, they were unable to adapt. The evidence was there for all to see: all the way up and down the convoy route were the green buoys marking the wrecks. True, some were from enemy action, but most were 'accidents'. He was glad that he had spent the day tightening up the convoy.

Meanwhile, all Steadfast could do was to wait as the merchantmen entered the most perilous part of their passage.

Chapter 15 – The Tragedy on the Buttercup

George Pickering, master of the *Buttercup*, sank back into his chair on the bridge, let out a long, deep sigh, and settled down to chew on his pipe. What a day it had been, he thought. Pickering was sixty years old, a short, thick-set, hardened seaman with a skin as tough as parchment and as dark as a pickled walnut. His eyes, narrowed by the years of staring across the sea, still had a sparkle about them, but his heavy movements betrayed the strain of his more than forty years on colliers. A lifetime of working for ship owners had left him resigned to life's vicissitudes, but tonight he was beginning to feel that he had had enough. After years of frugal living on land and hard living at sea, there was a tidy sum in his Newcastle Penny Bank account. More and more he found himself daydreaming of his allotment and the prizes he hoped to win at next year's county show. Although not unduly competitive, he was riled by only getting a second prize for his leeks this year. Next year he was determined on first prizes for leeks, carrots and onions.

'Hello, Chief. Up for a spot of air?'

'Yes. To tell the truth, I can't settle tonight. Not after today's shenanigans,' replied Gilroy McIntyre. Much the same age as Pickering, the Chief had no life beyond his engine room. He treated machinery like a friend – or sometimes like an unruly child – always expecting the best from his engines in return for the loving care of his skilful hands.

'I know what you mean. I'm a bit edgy myself.'

'Still, only another eight hours or so and we'll be home. My, am I looking forward to one of my wife's meat pies! Of course, what with the rationing, I don't ask her where she got the meat from.'

'We all have to look after number one these days. Best not to ask questions. Before the wife died she did a good Scotch pie.'

'Bad without her?'

'Aye. And it's worse with Angus being out in the desert. I hardly dare open the papers when there's news from Egypt.'

They fell silent as the *Buttercup* lumbered through the waves, low in the water with her heavy black cargo. Gilroy thought about the life he once had when he worked on the big liners, with their magnificent modern engines. He had given it up when Gladys became ill. They had had such a wonderful life until those last few years. First she went, then Angus was called up and now the war had dumped him in this filthy collier with engines that belonged on the scrap heap. Some days he wondered which was worse: the cold empty house in Wapping or the sweltering hellhole below.

'Not you as well, Sparks?' exclaimed Pickering.

'As well as what?'

'As us two that can't settle tonight.'

'Me neither. It's the thought of getting home to see Marjorie.'

'Oh, ho!'

Jack Brownlow didn't spend much time on the bridge or anywhere else except his cabin and the wireless room. He was the only youngster on the ship, and the only one who knew how to work the radio. He had learnt Morse code for a Scout's badge when he was at school, so when the war came he nagged his father into paying £30 a term for the Marconi Radio Officer course. His second class Post Master General ticket meant Marconi now paid him £8 a week. That was riches to Jack, who felt he was having a rather good war. Or, to be more precise, he and his girlfriend Marjorie were having a good war. They had met at the Regal Ballroom. Both mad about ballroom dancing, they were hoping to dance together for prizes soon. In fact, his friends said, Brownlow was having a *very* good war. As Pickering remarked to McIntyre, 'Young Brownlow thinks he's immortal. The young never think the bomb's got their name on it.'

***

McIntyre and Brownlow went below and Pickering took over the wheel from a seaman. He could think there as well as anywhere. Besides, they would be passing the northbound convoy soon. It was best to have a really experienced man at the wheel.

'Bloody mist,' complained Pickering, struggling to keep *Buttercup* in line with the *Patience* ahead of him. As he stared into the darkness he had a strange feeling that something was not right. *Patience* seemed too big, too dark.

Patience also seemed to be rather noisy tonight. Was something wrong with her? He strained his ears but could make no sense of the strange sound. Not to worry. Just keep to 7-knots and keep in line.

Pickering settled back into his relaxed homeward-bound mode, feeling quietly satisfied with *Buttercup*'s run on this convoy. He'd seen the planes that day and heard a lot of AA, but nothing near enough to worry about. Clapped out as *Buttercup* was, she had kept her 7-knots with disdainful disregard for Jerry and his antics.

He was jolted into action by the sound of churning water and the sensation of a massive looming shape in the darkness. It couldn't be *Patience* – she was too far ahead. But the mass was growing larger and was coming towards *Buttercup*. It seemed to be towering over him as if it was about to fall from the sky. He pressed the alarm and yelled, 'Ship on starboard bow!'

It was a straying oiler from the northbound convoy – all 8,000 tons of her.

Now Pickering could make out white streaks of foam at her bow, contrasting with the shapeless mass towering out of the water. He slammed the rudder over hard to port.

'Damn road hog! Well over the ruddy channel marker,' he muttered to himself.

But the mass of metal was still coming towards *Buttercup*, pounding and churning through the black sea, quite oblivious to the presence of Pickering's ship. Within seconds Pickering realised his evasion moves had failed. Collision was inevitable.

A surge of blind terror swept through the seaman as the *Buttercup* lurched sideways at the moment of impact. Instinctively he held on to the wheel and was saved from being hurled across the wheelhouse. He froze as his ears were lacerated by a long, loud screeching noise and a sound of straining metal as if a gigantic dentist's drill were ripping open the side of the ship. On and on went the stomach-churning rasping cacophony as the oiler ground into *Buttercup*'s beam, tearing, biting, grinding. Pickering looked aft to see gunnels and guardrails twisting off under the relentless forward juggernaut of the oiler. Bits of the deck were being rolled up like the lid of an opened sardine tin. The oiler dug deeper and deeper as she passed at an angle down the side of *Buttercup*. A boat exploded into a thousand splinters and disappeared on the wind. Sparks flew from the play of metal on metal.

The first smash had brought men rushing up from below. They stared in horror as the oiler ground her way down *Buttercup*'s side. Those men who had come up on the starboard side, fled the approaching monster. In the chaos a seaman tripped over a hosepipe and fell flat on the deck. The man behind him came down on top of him.

'Panickers,' hissed Pickering.

One of the newer arrivals, not yet inured to the hazards of convoy life, stood on the deck screaming and sobbing. The bosun grabbed him by the arm and tried to drag him below, but he froze to the spot in inconsolable terror.

Meanwhile, the northbound oiler, oblivious of the *Buttercup*, trudged past her and disappeared into the night.

Below, the cook had been thrown off his stool by the impact. The sickening sound of the heavy smash and the screeching metal had shaken every bone in his bulky frame, and a wave of icy fear ran through his body.

Pickering passed the wheel to a seaman – 'Just keep your eye on Patience' – and went aft to inspect the damage.

Not mortal, he thought, as he eyed the wrenched off stubs of the guardrails and the crumpled deck. It had been a glancing blow and *Buttercup* had taken it well. She looked a mess, but there was no reason to worry further tonight.

His sanguine thoughts were broken by the arrival of the Chief on deck.

'Plates are sprung, sir.'

'Badly?'

'Don't know yet, but there's water coming in.'

'Will they hold?'

'Hope so.'

'Well, get the pumps going and drop to 5-knots.'

Pickering returned to the bridge and cursed the night. At 5-knots they might miss the tide tomorrow and be stuck outside Tilbury for the next high tide. That was all extra cost to the owner – and cost was the only thing owners ever cared about.

Now *Buttercup* began to slowly slip behind the body of the convoy until an hour or so later she came level with the *Keswick* which was marking its rear. The hint of a grey dawn was breaking in the east, giving just enough light for Pickering to locate the corvette and guide *Buttercup* to within hailing distance. Picking up his megaphone he raised her bridge.

'We're stuck at 5-knots. Plates springing. We'll follow.'

'Good luck. You're on your own now,' came the reply from the *Keswick*.

As the corvette's stern disappeared into the half-dawn Pickering felt the loneliness of this moment. One wounded collier in a vast and hostile sea.

Roberts came back to the bridge.

'She's a tough one is our *Buttercup*,' he remarked in an attempt to show his lack of concern at their predicament.

Pickering, also reluctant to show any concern, responded: 'Yes. Remember that storm of '38?'

'That was a bad'un, that was. Hatches torn off and the waves crashing over. Couldn't see the deck most of the time. Never thought we'd get through that one.'

'We nearly didn't.'

'Aye. But this time it's no more than a few weeping rivets.'

As Pickering and Roberts sought to outdo each other with their uneasy reassurances, *Buttercup* seemed to stumble. Pickering called down to the chief.

'Everything OK, chief?'

'Not quite, sir. Shaft's running hot.'

'What revolutions can you get?'

'Don't rightly know, sir. Looks iffy.'

'Keep on it. We can't hang around here.'

Pickering was now seriously worried. The convoy would soon be far ahead. *Buttercup* was faltering in a vast, empty sea, but still within Jerry's hunting patch. If she ground to a halt they would have to radio for a tug – that would mean hours of playing the sitting duck in the middle of a war zone. With the arrival of daylight, reconnaissance planes could appear at any moment. His thoughts were interrupted by a wrenching, creaking sound from below. The voice pipe called.

'Yes, Chief.'

'The plates are giving, sir. I'm not sure the pumps can take it.'

'Can you keep up 3-knots?'

'So far, yes.'

'We need them.'

'Bosun, go below and report back on the plates.'

Several minutes passed. Pickering was calculating and recalculating. They were now about 50 nautical miles from Tilbury. At 8-knots they would be there in six or so hours. At 3-knots… that would be sixteen hours and the tide would be out. But he'd never failed to bring a ship home. He wasn't going to let this be the first.

At this moment the Bosun reappeared on the bridge.

'Looks bad, sir. There's rivets near to popping all along the starboard side.'

'Make up a shoring party and get to work.'

A dubious Bosun replied as firmly as he could, 'Aye, aye, sir,' and disappeared. He'd seen the plates, he'd seen how long and deep the damaged area was. They'd need to be carrying a forest of timber and have days of time to shore up that lot. But Roberts, like Pickering, had never failed to bring a ship home.

The shoring party gathered saws, hammers and nails and went below. In places the hull of the ship was dripping like a thawing hillside in spring. In other places rivulets of water were pouring into the hold and the lower rooms of the ship. Roberts picked out the worst leaks and put teams of two and three men to work on each. They didn't need telling how little time they had, nor the enormity of the task they faced. They worked furiously, exchanging only the few words necessary to coordinate their activity. One by one lengths of timber turned into props, which were rammed between the plates and any available fixture. Measure, cut, ram, hammer home… then secure with cross struts… On they went for an hour or so.

Roberts, who was working alongside the men, was keeping an eye on their progress. Some of the worst leaks had already been stopped, or at least reduced to a tolerable flow. A few more hours and the ship would, he hoped, be stabilised.

And then Roberts noticed it: the list. *Buttercup* had a list of ten or so degrees – far worse than when they had begun the shoring up. Somewhere there was an unseeable, unstoppable and lethal leak.

'Keep at it lads. I'll just have a word with the master.'

Pickering did not appear to be surprised to see Roberts. Indeed, he knew why Roberts was there.'

'The list?'

'Yes, sir.'

'Can you beat it?'

'No, sir. It's not from the plates we can see – it's somewhere else – probably behind the coal.'

'You mean you can't stop it?'

'No.'

'We'll see. We're still afloat and we are still doing 3-knots. Keep up the shoring.'

***

Half an hour later Pickering was surprised by a call of 'Ahoy there!' In his predicament he had not noticed the patrol ship coming up aft on his starboard bow.

'Need a tow?'

'That or a miracle,' shouted Pickering.

'Miracles not on offer today. Get ready to throw us a line,' came the trawler's response.

'Jones, Swinbrook, get a line ready forward.'

The Yorkshire Princess edged round the bows of the *Buttercup*. Swinbrook threw the coiled line across, where a waiting seaman caught it. It took fifteen minutes for Jones and Swinbrook to attach a heavy cable to the line and get it over to the trawler.

'All set?' called the trawler.

'All set,' replied Pickering.

The trawler edged forward to take up the slack and then began to increase speed to 3-knots, aided by *Buttercup* who was still running her own engines.

Pickering, reluctant to hand the wheel over at this critical time, kept an anxious eye on the cable. A sharp jerk was all that was needed for it to part and leave *Buttercup* alone once more.

He was also anxiously watching the list. It had grown to fifteen degrees while the tow was fixed up. He looked again. Twenty degrees!

'My God, she can't do it!' he muttered to himself.

Grabbing the megaphone he called up the trawler.

'How long to the nearest landing?'

'An hour or so, if you're desperate. Two hours if you want Harwich.'

'Desperate, please.'

Buttercup only had to hold for an hour – that sounded better than sixty minutes.

For the next twenty minutes Pickering watched as *Buttercup*'s list grew and grew… twenty five, thirty five. He pressed the alarm.

'Prepare to abandon ship.'

'Jones, Swinbrook, let go the cable!'

Men raced from below, clattering up the ladders to face the steeply sloping decks. Able seaman Johnson, a non-swimmer, panicked and threw himself onto the deck, failed to find a handhold, and slid down the wet plates to disappear into the sea.

The first two men to reach the securely lashed rafts were only able to stand up with difficulty. Ordinary seaman Butcher fumbled in his pocket for a knife to cut the lashings. In his panic he let go of the stanchion, fell backwards and joined Johnson in the deep. Gunner Harris was left by the raft but without a knife.

'Knife, somebody,' he yellowed.

'Catch,' yelled stoker Cunningham.

Harris caught the knife and hacked furiously at the raft. With only one hand to work with, he dropped the knife as soon as he had freed the raft and grabbed the line, pushing the raft behind him with his feet. The raft shot down the deck and settled on the light waves. Harris, who had held tight to the line, was yanked from his stanchion and bruisingly bounced down the deck into the water. A good swimmer, he stroked back to the ship to secure the line.

The second raft was even more troublesome. Neither able seaman Richards nor Stoker Davidson had a knife. Each needed one hand to stay upright so their one-handed efforts to untie the lashings proved hopeless. They tore their nails in their futile gripping of the knots, swollen by seawater.

'I'll get an axe,' cried Davidson and went across the perilous deck to reach a nearby locker. He seized a heavy axe but then faced dragging it across the slithery deck. 'Grab me by the waist,' he called to Davidson. With two hands free, one sharp, well-aimed chop at each lashing sent the raft tumbling down the deck, taking its line with it. Davidson let go of the axe and the two men followed the raft seawards.

By now almost all the men were in the water. Some had chosen their moment after first locating the rafts. Some had simply lost their balance and had been involuntarily thrown into the sea. Others had hesitated and attempted to cling to the ship until she left them no choice.

Two men remained. Hugging on to the jammed davit of the one remaining boat was young Jack Brownlow.

'I can't swim,' he cried.

From the rafts the men cried, 'Jump!' but Brownlow refused.

Not far from him was Pickering. He had sworn to bring the ship in but the sea had denied him that right. Never had he imagined that one of his ships would be under his feet and so near to her end. A proud career was being brought to an ignominious conclusion. Better to go down with the *Buttercup* than to live with the knowledge of this terrible day. And then he thought of his wife's meat pies, and jumped into the welcoming sea.

Buttercup turned over and with a rush of foaming sea and dirty spray slipped beneath the waves, taking Brownlow to his grave, so ending his hopes of a career as a ballroom dancer.

All that remained of *Buttercup* was a patch of boiling water and a miscellany of debris. Lifebuoys, oddments of timber, a pair of trousers, an oilskin and some charts slowly swirled round the spot where she had surrendered to the sea.

To one side of this patch of sad reminders of Pickering's ship were two life-rafts – one full, one barely occupied – and a number of struggling men. Few were good swimmers but most could dog-paddle well enough to reach a raft – except that the empty raft was drifting away from them. The bosun was the first man to reach it, only to find that there were no paddles. Leaning over the side he tried to paddle with his hands and steer the raft towards a group of men. First one, then two, then more men reached the raft and climbed in. With more hands to paddle, the raft moved more freely amongst the floating survivors. Soon it was full.

A dozen or more men were left in the water, some clinging to the sides of the rafts, some swimming gently round and round.

***

Of all the ships that sank on that convoy, *Buttercup* was the most fortunate. Within half an hour the patrol boat had located the two rafts and was hauling the cold, shocked survivors out of the water. Momentarily, Pickering forgot about his ship and dreamed of meat pies.

In turn, the Chief forgot about his engines as he consoled himself with the thought that Angus was not going to be an orphan after all.

Chapter 16 – The Return of the E-Boats

Steadfast heard nothing more of *Buttercup* after she had announced that she was dropping behind. He wondered if he should have ordered her into the nearest port but he knew how touchy the skippers were. Pickering ought to be able to look after himself after all those years, he thought. He settled down to enjoy the last few hours before the convoy could proceed alone up the Thames, and *Defiant* could peel off for Sheerness. Even Steadfast had had enough excitement for one convoy. But the enemy thought otherwise.

***

'Another day over – home tomorrow,' remarked Sherman as he handed over to Paris on the bridge at midnight.

'Anything happening?'

'No. It's so quiet you could go to sleep up here.'

'How's the convoy?'

'OK, I suppose, but you can't see a thing tonight.'

'Right. You can leave her to me.'

Sherman disappeared below, looking forward to a bit of sleep before a night out in London tomorrow.

'Starboard lookout: anything to report?'

'Nothing to report, sir.'

'Port?'

'Nothing to report, sir.'

'Let's hope it stays that way.'

About an hour later, and with a change of lookouts, a steward appeared on the bridge and handed Paris a mug of cocoa. Paris lifted the thick, sweet mixture to his lips and tentatively checked how hot it was. His anticipation of the warming drink was interrupted by a cry from a lookout:

'Motors on port bow!'

Paris lowered the mug and listened. There it was: the harsh, growling of an E-boat engine. His fist went for the alarm. A deafening hammering rattle shook every spar and plate of the ship. Sleeping men burst into life.

Those awake dropped tools, pencils, hands of playing cards. Boots, clothing, life-jackets and torches were snatched in an instant and a mass of men jostled their way down corridors and up ladders to action stations.

By this time Steadfast was on the bridge, glasses in hand, staring out in the direction indicated by the lookout. A faint sound of a faraway engine came drifting over the quiet sea.

'It's him!'

'Who, sir?'

'Korvettenkapitän Wendorff, of course.'

'How can you tell?'

'I've sensed it from the first day. He's out to get *Defiant*. That's why he's come back.'

'It doesn't really matter who it is, sir. It's all the same if we're hit.'

'Wendorff is different. He's more determined – and he's determined on this ship.'

'Why, sir?'

'Bit of a long story, but when my brother was killed the newspapers reported that I had sworn revenge on whoever did it. It was just chance that I later found out it was Wendorff – someone had been blabbing in a Portuguese café.'

'Had you really sworn revenge?'

'Yes, as it happens.'

'So you and Wendorff are in a sort of feud?'

'Something like that.'

'Helmsman, course oh-nine-oh.'

'Oh-nine-oh it is, sir.'

'Chief, half ahead.'

Defiant turned east and began to cut her way through the convoy. Paris looked on in petrified amazement. Neither he nor Steadfast could see the merchantmen and their masters had no idea that *Defiant* was about to cut across their bows.

'Wendorff's out there. He's given the challenge and I'm taking it,' said the emboldened commander.

Defiant sped through the waves for a few minutes before the wild frantic roaring of E-boat motors rent the calm of the convoy.

'E-boats ahead,' cried both lookouts almost simultaneously.

'Get him!' cried Steadfast, 'Guns, fire at will! Cole, commence zigzagging.'

Steadfast turned to Paris: 'He's dead ahead – just let him try and hit us now.'

A thunder of gunfire drowned the roar of the approaching E-boats, now clearly visible under the glare of star shells.

'Torpedoes ahead!'

Both Paris and Steadfast could see the torpedoes streaking through the sea, fine on the port bow. Cole was judging *Defiant*'s course with all the skill of a lifetime's ship-handling. He neatly slid away from the two phosphorescent trails. A cheer went up as the two torpedoes disappeared along *Defiant*'s beam.

While this action had been going on, the two outer E-boats had spread out, clearly hoping to pass on both sides of *Defiant*. But the one in the centre swung round and sped off to the east. Obviously he was out of torpedoes and so had to leave the battle area without delay.

It only took Steadfast a few seconds to realise that there was something wrong with that central boat. The engine roar was less aggressive than normal, and was somewhat irregular in its rhythm. 'She's damaged,' he said to himself.

'Full ahead, chief.'

Defiant was now racing after the central E-boat, her guns spewing fire and flame with all the fury that the ship could muster. Steadfast was oblivious to the merchantmen whose path he was crossing. To him the risk of slamming straight into the beam of a collier was nothing. As *Defiant* pursued her perilous hunt in the darkness, the battle area was illuminated only by a few star shells. The terrified lookouts searched the darker sea beyond for signs of approaching merchantmen. They now feared collision more than torpedoes.

On and on Steadfast drove *Defiant*, chasing the silvery wake of the crippled E-boat. Sometimes *Defiant* seemed to be gaining and the wake appeared larger and clearer. Then the distance between the two vessels lengthened and Steadfast called for more revolutions.

'Ship fine on the starboard bow,' called a lookout.

'Pass her to port, helmsman,' said Steadfast calmly.

A thundering sustained toot from the collier's siren provided the only comment on Steadfast's reckless manoeuvre. Meanwhile, all on the bridge held their breath as Cole conned the ship to pass less than 100 yards ahead of the collier.

'We're gaining on her,' remarked Steadfast a short while later, as the wake of the prey became obviously nearer.

'I wonder what they're thinking on that E-boat,' remarked Paris.

'Doubtless having a big row about tactics. Some for 'stay and fight' and some for 'flee and survive'. You can bet what you like that they're all swearing blue murder at their engineers. For once their famed engines are not going to get them out of trouble,' responded Steadfast.

Defiant was now gaining rapidly on the E-boat. Shell after shell blazed into the darkness, but somehow the boat continued unscathed. Then came a bright flash.

'A hit, sir!'

The E-boat seemed to jump in the water and a cloud of debris rose into the air.

'She's a gonner!' shouted Steadfast triumphantly. 'We've done for Wendorff!'

But then he heard the familiar and terrifying sound of the E-boat's engine as the vessel limped away into the darkness.

'Damn! She's only damaged!' cried Steadfast. Then, seeing his opportunity, and for once showing some excitement in battle, he cried out 'She'll never get away now. She's ours!'

The escaping E-boat could be heard dead ahead, her engines clearly not running at full power. Steadfast urged *Defiant* forward. All eyes and ears on the bridge were now trained in the direction of the fleeing enemy – the lookouts had abandoned their watch on the convoy. Steadfast knew that *Defiant* must now be crossing the northbound channel and was getting dangerously close to the British minefield.

Paris knew that too and was horrified as the ship carried them all nearer and nearer to the danger ahead. Finally he could no longer restrain himself:

'The minefield, sir?'

'We'll stop short, don't worry, Paris,' replied an excited and over-confident Steadfast.

Hardly had Steadfast finished reassuring Paris than he was thrown into the air and the ship shuddered from end to end. The lights went out.

The horrendous noise of the explosion had left everyone dumbfounded and disorientated, half expecting to find themselves injured or sinking into the sea. The men looked from one to another, as if seeking an explanation for the eruption. For a few moments a fearful silence descended on the stunned crew, broken only by the lapping of the water and the cries of the gulls overhead.

Steadfast turned to one of the lookouts: 'What was that, Roberts?'

'Not a torpedo, sir. Must have been a mine. The E-boats have all gone off.'

'Damn!'

The mine had first struck *Defiant* forward but did not immediately explode. Only after bumping along her bottom did it go off. Just what the damage was Steadfast did not yet know.

Steadfast turned to the engine-room voice-pipe: 'What's the damage, Chief?'

'Nothing serious, sir. She's blown a few fuses. Soon be fixed.'

Right, thought Steadfast. The engines are still turning and the electrics will be back soon, so we're not done yet.

There was also some smoke aft. Ross was already making his way towards the source, coughing and choking as he faced the clouds of hot vapour that now swathed the ship. Soon five men, eerily concealed by their breathing apparatus, were playing hoses on a fire that was coming up from a hole in the deck.

Able seaman Allsopp came up to the bridge: 'Report from Number One Sir. Serious damage to stern plates. Port screw missing. Nothing else vital.'

'Thank you, Allsopp.'

'Chief, how's things?'

'Electric's back. Ready to go when you are, sir.'

'Helmsman, course one-eight-oh.'

'Chief, port screw's gone. Slow ahead on starboard only.'

Paris turned to Steadfast, 'What now, sir?'

'Carry on. We can still do 7-knots.'

Steadfast inwardly cursed himself. He was certain that he had been chasing Wendorff, yet his enemy had got away and now the ship was damaged. Yes, but in the highest naval tradition of closing on the enemy.

No one could blame him for *that*, even if they were to blame him for straying into a British minefield.

***

Defiant rejoined the convoy and sailed on, looking more like a lumbering collier than a nimble war machine. Her burnt-out gun aft was now joined by a mass of tangled metalwork aft.

About half an hour later Allsopp was back with a fresh report from Gardiner: 'Bulkhead's damaged. Ship's taking on water.'

'Thank you. Ask Mr Gardiner to come to the bridge.'

Gardiner quickly returned.

'How bad is it?'

'I reckon we've taken on quite a bit of water. Now that the fire's more or less out, you can see there's a big rip in the bulkhead.'

'Umh. I thought we'd got off rather lightly for a mine. There's a chance that a good few bulkheads and plates have been weakened. Get a party onto it.'

Gardiner sent Phillips to put together a repair party.

Ten minutes later Phillips and a group of able seamen and gunners were at work on the bulkhead. They had sawn off half a dozen props and had put two in place when the catastrophe came.

Phillips, aided by Able Seaman Norman Owens, was manoeuvring a third prop into place when a grinding metallic sound filled their workspace. Before they could look for the source of the noise, a plate exploded from its rivets and a rush of water flooded into the compartment. The timbers already in place – not yet fully secured – were ripped from the bulkhead, which then burst. Phillips, Gunner Owens, Able Seaman Milner and Able Seaman Whitehead were washed off their feet. Owens got to his feet and struggled through the rapidly rising water to reach a watertight door. He quickly unlocked it but, even with Whitehead's help, there was no way the two men could open the jammed door.

Escape was now only possible through the emergency scuttle overhead. Phillips quickly unscrewed the clasps, noting with some surprise that the hatch was hot from the fire above. But when Phillips pushed the scuttle to open it, it stubbornly refused to move.

'The scuttle's jammed – won't budge.'

Each man tried pushing, hitting and shaking the scuttle, but there was not a sign of movement. Meanwhile the water had risen to their waists.

'The hammers!' cried Owens.

They had all dropped their tools when the flood first burst in on them. Owens couldn't swim, so Milner took a deep breath and dived down towards the deck. Phillips and Owens waited and waited. Milner shot into the air, his lungs bursting and his chest aching from the strain of the dive.

'Can't... see... the... hammers,' he gasped.

Rogers immediately dived into the ever rising flood. All that the others could see was his feet, still shod, waving above the water. He too seemed to spend an astounding length of time under water. When he shot back up, Owens, Milner and Whitehead could see that he too had not located the hammers.

Down went Milner again. His companions waited. Up came Milner. Too exhausted to speak, he simply shook his head and disappeared again. Another wait, relieved by first a hammer, then a hand, and then Milner rushing up from below. Milner, now almost doubled-up by the agonies of his time under water, collapsed into Phillips's arms. Whitehead seized the hammer just as it was about to slip from Milner's grasp.

The water was nearing shoulder height as Whitehead attacked the scuttle with the furious hammer blows of a despairing man. It was hard to get the angle right – hammering on a deckhead is not easy, even at the best of times. But his mortal dread of the rising water drove him on as wild blow followed wild blow. Suddenly the scuttle burst open and a rush of air from the deck reminded the men of the safe haven that awaited them above. Whitehead climbed into the scuttle and disappeared.

'What are we going to do about Milner?' asked Owens.

'We'll have to take him between us. You go first and take his hand. I'll push from behind.'

Try as they would, neither man had the strength to manhandle Milner up the small rungs of the escape shaft. Milner was unconscious and a deadweight.

'You go,' said Rogers.

'But...'

'Go! They'll need you on deck.'

Owens hesitated, his face showing the agony of the moment.

'Go! Go!' screamed Rogers.

Owens clambered into the shaft, feeling like a criminal.

Rogers held Milner upright as long as he could, slapping his face and shouting 'Come on Milner! You can make it!' No response came.

As the water rose towards Rogers's chin, he kissed Milner on the forehead and gently let him slide into the water. With tears in his eyes, he grasped the first rung of the scuttle ladder.

Rogers, dripping with water and in a shocked state, climbed up to report to the bridge.

'How's the shoring up going?' asked Steadfast.

'Too late. We're flooded aft – should be OK if the door holds. But Milner's gone, sir. Couldn't make it out aft.'

'Too bad.'

***

Rogers turned to leave the bridge. As he reached the ladder the ship was lifted bodily by a gigantic explosion forward. Steadfast was knocked sideways, hit his head on the binnacle and fell stunned to the deck. Ross was thrown across the bridge and Rogers lost his footing, slid sideways and disappeared. A good part of the bow had been shorn off with the explosion of the forward magazine – a delayed response to the mine's first point of impact on the ship.

When Steadfast came round he saw Ross clinging to the bridge rail as if his life depended on it.

For the moment the ship was suspended in a terrified silence.

Chapter 17 – The End of Defiant

'Cole, go forward and check the damage,' ordered Steadfast.

Cole tore down ladders and rushed along corridors to the forward stores area. He was ankle-deep in water long before he had reached the cable locker. Not much further ahead he could see a mangled watertight door, drunkenly hanging on one hinge and twisted back. Flames were licking round its edges – flames from an intense and deadly fire.

He rushed back to the bridge to communicate the fatal news. 'Fire in the forward magazine, sir. Watertight door's blown as well – nothing to keep the fire back.'

'How long can we stay afloat?'

'Don't rightly know, sir. Depends.'

'On what.'

'On putting out the fire and just hoping there ain't a big hole forward that we can't get at.'

'Very well, Cole, resume course.'

Cole once more noticed Steadfast's unflappable style of command. After all, he thought, Steadfast must have realised that an explosion like that would have caused substantial damage forward – for now masked by the fire. But for how long? No one, not even Steadfast could imagine that *Defiant* was going to survive for more than an hour or two.

'Engine room, half ahead,' called Steadfast calmly.

Defiant settled back into the convoy. She only needed to keep 7-knots. Injured as she was, her engines were undamaged and were still able to force her mangled bow through the light sea without difficulty. But the smoke billowing from the forward magazine area hinted of the danger she was in. Above, puffy cumulus congestus clouds were dotted round the blue sky. Below the grey sea was at last calm. Steadfast watched the convoy and admired its reasonably tight formation. He'd done a good job of herding it back into shape. There was no reason to suspect that anything would disturb these last few hours to parting off Sheerness – other than *Defiant*'s bow, of course.

What is the difference between putting on a brave face and plain delusion? Few on *Defiant* would have cared to answer that question that afternoon. The ship was in a worse shape than any vessel still in the convoy. There was water coming in fore and aft, a few men lost and some wounded below. For now Steadfast was treating all this damage as just proud battle scars. If he could only bring *Defiant* back to port, all would be well.

'List ten degrees, sir.'

'Very good, Number One. Keep an eye on it.'

Ten degrees wasn't much in a calm sea and so near to port, thought Steadfast. When he was a lieutenant on HMS Staffordshire they'd crawled into Malta with a twenty-five degree list and a large part of the superstructure shot away. *Defiant* would be alright as long as she wasn't asked to do any sharp turns – the Admiralty's endless piling of new gadgets up top was making the destroyers a bit top-heavy nowadays.

Steadfast was not the only one who was thinking about the list. Down below it was just about the only topic of conversation. Phillips had been boring his fellow seamen with his 'new captain' ever since Steadfast had set foot on the gangway. The state of the ship only led him to more and more portentous declarations:

'See, not just a new captain, but one who doesn't know when 'e's beat. Look at that.'

Phillips pointed to a tumbler of water on the mess room table, vividly showing the list as if it were a builder's level.

'Half-a-crown the glass falls off the table before the captain declares "Abandon ship".'

'Done,' cried Signalman Roberts, 'e's a stubborn bastard, but not that suicidal.'

***

Half an hour later the tumbler fell to the deck and Roberts forfeited his half-a-crown. Meanwhile the firefighters were losing their battle with the forward fire, which was gradually crawling aft along the ship. To add to *Defiant*'s troubles, the list was continuing to grow.

On the bridge no money had been placed on the list, but Gardiner and Steadfast were both preoccupied with the state of the vessel. The commander was willing to do almost anything to keep *Defiant* with the convoy, but Gardiner was in a more realistic mood.

'Time to go, sir?' asked Number One, 'no one will get off the starboard side now, and port is getting tricky.'

Secretly cursing his luck, Steadfast turned to the Coxswain: 'Pipe abandon ship, Mr Coxswain.'

The order rang out over the ship. Roberts was not the only man to have been discussing this call for the last half hour. Most of the crew had been listening for it ever since the list had passed fifteen degrees.

Just at the moment that Phillips had piped the order, the ship gave a strange lurch and seemed to settle lower aft. It was the signal for pandemonium.

Most of the men panicked and, hardly had the last echoes of the order died away than many were in the water, swimming frantically away from the ship. Others just froze, neither daring to jump nor searching for the survival gear. One young seaman had collapsed on deck, screaming and crying with terror, resisting all attempts of his mates to get him to leave the ship.

Only a few were disciplined enough to remember the abandon ship routine. One man was slashing away with a knife at the bindings on a Carley float. The last binding went and, holding the line tightly, he grabbed the raft and threw it over the side. Others fell upon lengths of timber, whaleboat gear and other floatable objects, and cast them into the sea. Scrambling nets were thrown down the ship's side and lifebuoys with heaving lines attached were hurled into the sea. Some men clambered down the nets, others more or less walked off the sinking ship onto the rafts. Soon the port side of ship was a mass of bobbing heads, waving arms and drifting rafts.

Ralph Metcalfe, a cook, dropped down into the sea and swam uneasily to the nearest raft. As he reached it, he heard yells of, 'We're full!' He grabbed a lifeline attached to the raft and hung on tight. Stoker Herbert Palmer was not far behind him. Hearing the cry, he began to swim in a slow circle around the raft – he was more likely to be rescued near a raft than alone on the wider sea.

Defiant had a good few non-swimmers and others who simply feared leaving the solidity of the ship. They stood, lined up along the side and watched as some of the rafts, not yet full, paddled away. 'Wait for us… bastards!' A faint call of, 'Jump!' came from one raft as it continued to move away to avoid being sucked down by the vortex of the ship's sinking.

Steadfast and his officers were still on board *Defiant*. Seeing the chaos on deck and in the sea, the commander ordered Gardiner to take charge of the men on deck. Then he ordered Paris and Beverton to each commandeer a raft and start organising the collection of the men.

Amidst the panic and chaos, some men had kept their heads and remembered their routines. The Chief had heard nothing from Steadfast, so he opened the safety valves – he didn't fancy being the one who ended the ship by blowing up her boilers.

Phillip's mind was also concentrated on the abandon ship routine. He found a bunch of keys in the Boatswain's cabin and went off to the safe. He tried one key after another until finally the door clicked open. He collected all the confidential papers, books and cash, locked the empty safe, and went to the nearest fuel tank access, and dropped the papers in. The cash went into his pocket. Maybe it could stay there, he thought. He chuckled at his locking the safe. If the ship didn't go down, some poor German might spend hours trying to open it, only to find it empty.

Some men kept their heads enough to rescue precious items. Petty Officer Dennis Kellaway snatched his ditty box before running up to the deck. One look at the cold water and the chaos of boats, floats and men was enough for him to jettison the box. First, though, he opened it, took out his wife's photo and stuffed the picture in a pocket. Then he reluctantly dropped the box and plunged into the cold mêlée below.

For some, the prospect of the freezing sea was beyond imagining. Ordinary seaman Eric Sullivan sat on the steeply sloping deck, screaming and crying loudly. When Sick Berth Attendant Leslie Carpenter and Leading Wireman Clarence Horton tried to help him, he seemed not to notice their presence. On and on he gibbered and cried, shaking uncontrollably. They tried to lift him towards the gunwale, but he simply grabbed a railing and held on with a vice-like grip. Nothing would move him. They turned away and slid down the deck to face the peril that Sullivan could not accept.

Leading Seaman Warren Armstrong and Able Seaman Wilbert Parsons had gone straight to their post at the davits of the port boat when the call came to abandon ship. They had practised this so many times but now came the test when seconds counted while all around them were men facing death. They quickly cut the inboard mooring ropes and hauled the boat up out of its chocks – a task made easier by the absence of the guardrails that had been lost in the storm. The two strong men – this was a job for only the toughest of the sailors – winched the davits outboard until the boat hung clear of the ship. On an exercise they would have taken the boat down to deck level and let the men board her before dropping down to the sea. As the *Defiant* listed ever more, there was no time for such gentilities. Armstrong and Parsons leapt into the boat and lowered it by the falls. There was no one in the boat to fend off the *Defiant*, so they did their best, each standing on one leg and shoving off with the other. Years of training showed as the boat remained level and dipped gently into the sea. The two men looked at each other and exchanged modest nods of mutual satisfaction.

'That'll show the lieutenant,' said Parsons.

Filling the boat was another matter.

Freed from the falls the boat now rose and fell on the sea. One minute it was bumping into the ship's side; the next the sea was sucking it away to leave a perilous gap. A safe jump from the deck above required careful timing. The first man to go heeded Parson's 'Jump!' and landed plumb in the middle of the boat. Gervass came to the edge of the ship. Parsons shouted, 'Now!' Gervass started forward as if to obey the shout, hesitated, teetered back, then jumped. His hesitation had been just long enough for the sea to suck the boat away. He fell into the gap between boat and sea, smashing his shoulder on the boat's gunwale. Next came the portly chief steward. Not agile on his feet at the best of times, he could neither find the courage to jump nor the quickness to go at the right moment. So many times he forced his stocky frame forwards, and so many times he pulled back. When he finally went he had lost all control. The boat was rushing back towards the ship and crushed him between boat and ship.

What should have been an orderly loading of the boat turned into a frantic effort to heave men out of the water. First came the uninjured, who could help themselves over the side. Then came the delicate task of pulling in the injured Gervass. Of Peters, there was no sign.

Parsons and Armstrong then rowed around, picking up survivors still in the water. Soon the boat was dangerously overloaded.

In the chaos of *Defiant*'s end, some men escaped by chance, some with difficulty. Others perished in the doomed ship.

George Barton was in his wireless cabin when the magazine went up. He stepped out on hearing the massive explosion and saw some smoke and flames but no other serious damage. He returned to his messages. Reception was bad that day and Barton was tired from the labours of last night. He put his headphones on, opened a code book and began to work on his next message. Perhaps it was the fumes from below, perhaps plain exhaustion, but when the first flames began to reach the wireless cabin, Barton was already slumped over his desk.

Ordinary seaman Alfred Davies first noticed the fire around the wireless cabin. It seemed to burst from underneath with little warning, quickly engulfing the room. He seized a hose and pointed its powerful jet on the base of the flames. Suddenly he felt the flow weaken. With a gurgle and a spatter the flow dropped to a trickle. The pump had failed. Barton and his cabin roared to extinction.

Stoker 1st class James Summers was on his way up top when he heard cries from a cook. He was trapped in a small store room. The door was jammed and he was shouting through a small scuttle in the door. Summers ran to help. He tore at the door, kicked it, shook the handle… nothing would move it. Beneath him the water was rising, while his lungs were filling with ever denser smoke. He gave one last pull on the door, but still it would not move. Summers thrust his hand through the scuttle and shook the cook's hand, 'Best of luck, Ralph.' Then he fled up to the main deck, tears running down his face.

***

With most of the men off the ship, a quiet calm descended on the scene. The *Defiant*, still listing twenty-five degrees, sat in the water, apparently scorning the predictions of her imminent sinking. The overloaded boat was dipping up and down in the choppy sea and two crammed rafts were idly drifting. The only sounds came from the rise and fall of the sea, the cries and moans of injured men, and the calls of men searching out their mates. A few lifeless bodies drifted with the swell. From time to time the muffled tolling of a distant buoy rang out like the toll of a funeral bell.

But it was the smell that the men were to remember. Fuel oil lay in a thick layer on the water. Its vapour filled men's nostrils, its acrid chemicals scoured their lungs and stung their throats. Their eyes itched and smarted, their mouths were raw and their stomachs wretched. Oil had become their enemy as much as had the sea.

Nor did it take long for the piercing, numbing cold to penetrate the men's bodies. Those clinging to ropes had to force life into frozen hands.

Whitehead could hear his best friend Sullivan calling in the dark. They had enlisted together after school and been in the Navy since 1937. It was only on the *Defiant* that they found themselves reunited. Thoughts of their endless football games on the waste patch behind the scrap metal yard in Goddard Street flooded into his head. He called back, 'Hang on, Eric, I'm coming.' He set off in the direction of the cry, trying to keep his head above the oil-covered water, and pushing his way through the debris from the ship. When he reached the area where he thought Eric was, there was no sign of him. Nor did he hear another cry from his friend.

All that the survivors could do was to wait. Sparks must have sent out an SOS call, they all said, but the wait seemed an eternity in this hostile sea. Anyway, they were still in the swept channel. Something would come by soon.

Steadfast was still on the bridge and Gardiner on the deck as the last man went over the side. Steadfast had watched the crew's chaotic abandoning of the ship with growing dismay. His first impression three days ago had been right: they were an undisciplined lot. If only he had had more time to put some order and routine into the ship. But there was no more time. Her end was near, as was his first command.

He reached for his lifejacket and put it over his head and blew into the valve. The jacket remained as flat as yesterday's party balloon. He took the jacket off and inspected it. Several sizeable gashes from flying splinters had rendered it unusable. He looked around the bridge for a spare. Not a jacket in sight. 'Damn! My bloody fault for complaining so much about keeping the ship tidy.' There was no time to search for another jacket. He snatched a sorbo cushion and shoved it under his coat. Not a very dignified way to leave the ship, he thought.

Steadfast knew that now he had to leave, but only as the last man.

'Number One, would you leave now, please.'

'But, sir...'

'There's nothing more you can do.'

Gardiner clambered down the netting and slipped into the freezing water.

It was time for a last check for survivors. Steadfast went down below and searched as far as the water permitted – which was not very far. Then he checked all the cabins and gun enclosures. No one. All that remained was for him to slide the few feet down into the sea. Without a backward glance he swam to the nearest life raft and reached for a line.

Chapter 18 - Rescue

There had been no SOS from Sparks, but the Yeoman Signaller's aldis lamp had passed the distress call down the convoy until it reached Lieutenant Commander Waldridge on the *Keswick*. How many survivors were in the water he did not know, but Waldridge couldn't even risk going to find out. The *Keswick* was all the protection that the convoy had left. He reported the apparent sinking back to the coastal forces.

Over one hundred men had gone over the side of *Defiant* and now they were variously spread out in the boat, on rafts, clinging to rafts or floating around them. Steadfast was in the water and swam from raft to raft to reassure his men that help would soon arrive. But he knew that some men were already beyond help. Several had severe burns with large areas of skin peeling away. The burns victims seemed to have passed the first stage of searing pain and were now in deep shock: grey, motionless and shivering. Some were weakly calling for water.

Elsewhere he could see men with gashed heads, smashed arms and chest wounds. He knew that hidden below the dark water there would be smashed legs and broken pelvises.

On one raft Kendrick was bent over a man with huge wounds, doing what he could with a few bits of lint and a roll or two of bandage. Gibbs was on the other raft bandaging a man who had lost an eye.

'I knew 'e was bad news,' said Greenwood, floating near Elphick in the dark sea. 'E chased that E-boat near enough into the minefield. *Our* minefield! Can't tell the difference between hunting down one of his foxes and messing with mines.'

'What a bastard!' responded Elphick.

'Better be his last bloody command.'

'Don't you bank on it. He sent two E-boats to the bottom. That'll be enough to put him back on a bridge.'

'So what does he have to do for their Lordships to put him into pen pushing?'

'Haven't a clue, but he'll get another ship. I'll put a week's rum ration on it.'

'Done. Pity the poor sods who sail with him.'

Able seaman Allsopp paddled over to the two men.

'Where's Hancock?'

'He was near us a while back,' replied Elphick.

'Hancock! Hancock!' – There was no reply.

Elphick paddled off and took a look at some of the men nearby. He found Hancock and shook and slapped him, desperately shouting: 'Hancock! Wake up! Wake up!' There was no response.

'He's gone,' called out Elphick.

Others went, too, in the freezing water as they waited for dawn and the hope of rescue.

Death on the rafts was more obvious. You could tell when a man went. A strange stillness – no breath, no twitches, no moans or sighs – would come over him. On Phillips's raft, Slingsby, Carpenter and Summers all went, one by one. Each dead man was tipped over into the sea and the cry, 'Room for one more!' would go up.

Whether it was colder in the sea or on the rafts, no one could tell. Everyone knew about the numbing agony of the icy sea, but the rafts had their own torment. The cold waves splashed up on the men and the freezing wind sucked every spark of warmth from their bodies.

Ross was on a float with about twenty men. At first they had talked, then the talk subsided to a low chatter, but now, after an hour, the float was strangely quiet. 'The men are going,' he thought. He was determined to keep them conscious.

'Right, lads, we've got to keep awake. It's time for a song!'

He struck up, 'Come all ye young fellows that follow the sea / to my way haye, blow the man down,' but the men left the first verse to him.

'Come on lads, second verse,' and he struck up a faltering 'I'm a deep water sailor just in from Hong Kong'.'

The men began to sing. It was hard work, but Ross kept them at it. After a while, one man, and then another, volunteered their own choice of songs.

***

With the first greyness of dawn, hope and despair alternated on the floats, on the boat and in the sea. Some men saw the half-light as a sign of rescue to come. Some saw only the numerous lifeless bodies drifting on the debris-strewn sea, and felt nothing but despair.

'A ship!' cried Gibbs.

It was fortunate that Ross's raft had some dry flares. He lit one and its billowing red smoke soared over the desperate survivors.

Within minutes it was clear that the ship was coming towards the rafts. When perhaps a mile away, Ross felt it safe to use one more of the precious flares to confirm their position. The sight of the flare's powerful pyrotechnic display roused a cheer in the traumatised men and a few began once more to talk to neighbours.

The patrol ship HMS *Arundel* came into sight, scrambling nets already down on both sides. Those in the water still able to swim quickly made their way over to the ship and were helped up the nets by ready hands. One by one the near lifeless men floating in the water were pulled into the boat and the men carried over to the *Arundel*. Several of the injured were taken up in cradles. Then the rafts were towed to the ship and the men hauled up onto *Arundel*'s deck.

***

Steadfast had been the last off the ship and was the last to go up the nets to the safety of *Arundel*'s crowded deck. As he came over the gunwale he straightened up and surveyed what was left of *Defiant*'s complement. All the officers? Yes. Chief Petty Officer? Yes. Quartermaster? Yes.

'Christ!' he yelled, 'Elton, where's Elton?'

Cries of, 'Not here,' came from some of the huddles on the deck.

'Hell! He's still locked up on *Defiant*! I'm going back.'

'Phillips, Cole, can you take me over?'

Both men were not used to a *request* from their commander, but realised the guilt implicit in Steadfast's appeal. Elton was Steadfast's prisoner and it was *he* who had forgotten him when he gave the order to abandon ship.

Phillips and Cole glanced over to the flaming *Defiant*. The fire was no more than one-third of the way down the ship so Elton was well clear of danger for the moment.

'Of course, sir,' they replied in a condescending tone which fully conveyed their delight in the commander being under an obligation to them.

Steadfast turned to Lieutenant Commander Railton, *Arundel*'s captain: 'May we borrow your boat for a while, Captain? I can't ask any of your men to risk their necks in this one.'

'It's yours to command, Steadfast. I wish you luck.'

The boat was still in the water. Steadfast, Phillips and Cole clambered down the nets and boarded the craft. Phillips and Cole shipped the surplus oars and then rowed the short distance over to *Defiant* with Steadfast at the tiller.

'We'll go for that net aft,' he explained.

Fortunately the wind was blowing the flames towards *Defiant*'s prow so there was little risk in tying up to the net aft.

As Steadfast prepared to climb the net, he turned to his oarsmen:

'You two stay here. I've got a whistle. One blast means I've got Elton and I'm on my way back. Two blasts means I can't get back and you're to scarper. Read that back.'

The two men repeated Steadfast's code and the commander romped up the net and disappeared over the shattered gunwale.

Defiant's list was now about thirty-five degrees and the deck was covered in oily water plus the debris of the explosion. Each step that Steadfast took towards the lock-up where Elton had been since last night was a hazard in itself. Without a handhold he would slip back down the deck, so each move had to be planned with the greatest care, as if he were rock climbing on a particularly difficult face. Several times he slithered back a few steps when the bits of wire, rope and remnants of fittings came away in his hands. Each foot gained was bought at the cost of further lacerations to his now bleeding hands.

'Elton, are you there?'

'Yes, sir, what's happening?'

'Abandon ship – I'm coming to get you.'

When Steadfast reached the lock-up he took one look at the gigantic Royal Naval issue padlock and cursed the Navy's efficiency. Only a deck axe would get that off, he thought.

It took several minutes for Steadfast to slither sideways along the deck to the nearest axe, and even longer to get back to Elton without dropping the heavy instrument. All the while, the heat of the creeping fire reminded him of the peril that the two men were now in.

'I've got it, Elton. Stand back while I smash the lock.'

As Steadfast poised the raised axe to strike the blow that would release Elton, he felt *Defiant* shudder. The axe smashed down on the lock, which flew into the air just as *Defiant* lurched sharply in the direction of her list. Steadfast lost his foothold, the axe fell from his hand, and he slid down the deck back into the sea. His first instinct was to attempt to re-board the ship and complete his rescue of Elton. The damaged gunwale was now under water so Steadfast searched around for something to hold onto while he pulled himself up. After seizing a rather rough bit of damaged rail with his raw and bleeding hands, he began to attempt to pull his tired body up once more onto his dying ship. Barely had he begun to lift himself, when *Defiant* gave another shudder. She was rolling over!

Steadfast let go and slipped into the water. Lying on his back, he kicked off against the moving deck of *Defiant* as hard as did his hunter when enraged by a yapping dog. He shot off from *Defiant*'s rolling carcass and neatly turned over in order to swim away from the ship. But his failing strength was no match for the sucking forces of *Defiant*. He disappeared beneath her gurgling vortex.

When Steadfast surfaced again his lungs were bursting. His heart pounded and his diaphragm beat like an out of control bass drum as his body cried out for air. When he had gathered enough strength to look around, all that he could see at first was the near to being upturned hull of *Defiant*. But no sign of Elton.

Phillips and Cole were still in the boat, waiting for Steadfast to return, or the two whistle blasts that would order them to flee. Steadfast had not been in view when he first boarded *Defiant* so they were unaware that a new disaster was unfolding. They noticed the first shift in *Defiant*'s list but thought little of it. So when the second shudder came, with the sudden switch to a roll, they were caught off guard.

'She's rolling!' yelled Cole.

'Hell, she's going under!' responded Phillips.

'Cut the painter!' screamed Cole from his end of the boat. Phillips fumbled in pockets, pulled out a knife and opened the blade. As the knife met the rope, *Defiant* made her final roll, taking the boat down into the deep. Phillips and Cole, still in her, disappeared.

Steadfast had no idea of what was happening to Cole and Phillips. His whole mind was focused on Elton. He searched for any sign of him amongst the debris. There he was, clinging to a plank.

'Elton, I'm coming,' yelled Steadfast as he struck out towards the bobbing figure.

But Elton did not hear him. He was too far gone from a blow on head when he tumbled down *Defiant*'s deck into the sea. Silently, unhurriedly, his grip on the plank weakened and he slipped beneath the waves.

Steadfast did not notice Elton go. The salt, the oily water and the choppy waves blurred all that he saw. So when he reached the abandoned plank he was overcome by a wave of panic. Elton was his prisoner. *He* had ordered his locking-up. And *he* had forgotten about him. All his triumphs over the E-boats would be forgotten once people heard that Elton had gone.

In desperation, for his own sake rather than Elton's, Steadfast dived under the plank. He could see little, so he swung his arms from side to side and up and down but found nothing. Choking and spluttering he came to the surface again. Then his aching lungs responded once more to his demand for a deep breath. Down he went. Now he was flailing his arms even more desperately, but his strength was ebbing fast. His lungs finally refused to endure any more torture and he shot to the surface, gasping, retching and with every blood vessel in his head and neck throbbing to within a fracture of bursting.

Steadfast lay exhausted and dejected as the sea tossed his shattered body up and down and from side to side. He could see the *Arundel* in the distance and knew that the men on her deck would be watching these last moments of *Defiant*. He turned to swim back to *Arundel*.

As he kicked back in the water, his left foot hit something. 'Elton!'

Down went Steadfast, newly energised with the hope of saving the seaman. He grabbed him by the jacket with his left hand and struck out with his right arm to bring them both to the surface. For a moment he rested, holding Elton's head clear of the water. Then he moved off towards an abandoned raft.

At the raft Steadfast first tried to push the deadweight of Elton up onto it, but as soon as he had lifted Elton more than a foot or so, the lifeless weight fell back into the sea. Next he tried to haul himself onto the raft while still clinging to Elton. A few attempts were enough to prove this impossible. He fell back into the sea, resolving to cling to Elton and perhaps tow him towards *Arundel.*

By now Steadfast was too exhausted to keep himself alive, let alone Elton. He was on the point of abandoning his charge when a discarded lifejacket floated by. He grabbed it. Lying on his back with Elton's floating head towards him, Steadfast inched the jacket over each of Elton's arms and then tied the strings. He let go: Elton was floating.

From the moment of the second shudder to the disappearance of Steadfast, Phillips, Cole, and Elton had been a matter of seconds. Seconds that held the men on the *Arundel* in frozen awe at the sight of the unfolding catastrophe. They were powerless to help and there was no other boat in the water to go to the aid of *Defiant's* victims. All they could do was watch as Steadfast struggled with the released prisoner.

There was a cheer as Steadfast put the lifejacket round Elton, but a gasp of horror at what followed. The exhausted Steadfast had expended his last ounce of energy. His head slumped forwards and disappeared beneath the waves.

The crew of *Arundel* rushed to lower a second boat. Hardly had they reached it when Gardiner cried out, 'The captain!' Steadfast's apparently motionless body had bobbed up from the deep.

Gardiner threw off his jacket, tore off his sea boots and dived the ten feet or so from the *Arundel's* deck into the churning sea. All on the deck of the *Arundel* were stunned into a combination of silent admiration and bewildered surprise at Gardiner's foolhardy action. But as Gardiner's powerful crawl carried him nearer and nearer to the drifting captain, a murmur of approval spread amongst the men. And when they saw him reach Steadfast and turn to drag him back, a cheer went up. The nearer that Gardiner got to the *Arundel*, the louder the cheer became.

Gardiner's return had been anticipated and some men from the *Arundel* were already at the bottom of the net ready to haul him and his captain up. Gardiner dropped down onto the deck, exhausted but with an inner sense of vindication. The RNVR had shown its mettle.

The boat that went out after Phillips, Cole and Elton soon found the three men. Elton was in poor shape but the Chief Petty Office and the Coxswain were unharmed beyond being wet and cold.

By the time that the *Arundel* was ready to return to Harwich, all that remained of *Defiant* was the sad flotsam of spars, shreds of clothing and shattered remnants of furniture.

Meanwhile Steadfast was below receiving the attention of Kendrick. Apart from his lacerated hands he was uninjured and his soaking already seemed a thing of the past.

Half an hour later, as the *Arundel* sped back towards port, Steadfast asked to see Gardiner. Gardiner had no idea what to expect. Was he to be the recipient of over-fulsome thanks from a guilty captain? Was Steadfast about to prime him on how to present the last few days as an outstanding victory over the foe? Did Steadfast want him to pass on a reassuring message to a relative? The truth was most unexpected:

'I've been thinking, Number One,' said the commander, now sitting up in a bunk, 'are you the Gardiner that won a swimming medal at the 1928 Olympics?'

'Yes, sir.'

'I think I may have underestimated you – and the RNVR, Gardiner.'

'Kind of you to say so, sir.'

***

Meanwhile, Phillips and Cole were drinking hot cocoa in a mess a few feet away from the captain. Phillips could not help thinking about his conversation with George Barton just a few days ago.

'I was right,' Phillips said.

'About what?' asked Cole.

'This being the captain's first ship. I warned that young Barton, but he just laughed it off.'

'What did you tell him?'

'That it's bad luck to be on a captain's first ship.'

'Well, it was certainly bad luck being on this one.'

'You could always trust Smithy to know just how far to push his luck with Jerry.'

'Yes, he got it just right. This captain's too fond of a scrap. Too much of a medal hunter.'

'What do you think he'll get for this run? A reprimand or a gong?'

'If they've any respect for the men, they'll give him a right dressing down. But my money's on a gong for the E-boats.'

'And us?'

'A mug of hot tea and a currant bun.'

Naval Terms

RN - A career naval officer.

RNR - A professional seaman who volunteered to join the reserve.

RNVR - A civilian who voluntarily does part-time naval training.

23901330R00066

Printed in Great Britain
by Amazon